HOSTAGE OF THE HITMAN

ALEXIS ABBOTT

PATHFORGERS PUBLISHING

© 2016 **Pathforgers Publishing.**

All Rights Reserved. This is a work of fiction. Names, characters, places and incidents are the product of the author's imaginations. Any resemblances to actual persons, living or dead, are entirely coincidental.

This book is intended for sale to Adult Audiences only. All sexually active characters in this work are over 18. All sexual activity is between non-blood related, consenting adults. This is a work of fiction, and as such, does not encourage illegal or immoral activities that happen within.

Cover Design by Wicked Good Covers. All cover art makes use of stock photography and all persons depicted are models.

More information is available at Pathforgers Publishing.

Content warnings: kidnapping, Stockholm Syndrome, mafia violence, BDSM

Wordcount: 65,000 Words

Get an EXCLUSIVE book, **FREE** just as a thank you for signing up for my newsletter! Plus you'll never miss a new release, cover reveal, or promotion!

http://alexisabbott.com/newsletter

PART OF ALEXIS ABBOTT'S HITMAN
SERIES

READING ORDER:

Don't miss out on the rest of the Hitman Series by Alexis Abbott! Now available on all ebook retailers, in paperback format, and now becoming available in audiobook!

Owned by the Hitman
Sold to the Hitman
Saved by the Hitman
Captive of the Hitman
Stolen from the Hitman
Hostage of the Hitman
Taken by the Hitman

PROLOGUE

I've had the wounded bird with me for some time, but it's been clear for a while she's ready to fly once more. She's grown accustomed to my hold, after all my time tending her. She doesn't struggle, doesn't try to fly away. Her shiny red breast gleams in the light through the train window.

I open up the sliding window, and feel the air get sucked out. The little bird hops about the table before me, chirping excitedly. She's unsure of what to do, even looks back at me. And I can't help but smile. Poor creature; once upon a time she tried to fight my care. But she'd be dead without it. Now it's hard for both of us to accept it as the scenery of southern France flies by. I give her a gentle nudge and she zips away, vanishing into the picturesque countryside. She'll be fine, but I'll miss the noisy girl.

She wouldn't have wanted to see what I need to do next.

The Mediterranean coast spans the other side of the cabin's view. We'll be reaching the Spanish border before much longer, and that means it's time to act.

Watching the view of the water outside disappear behind lush forest, I slowly fold up my napkin from the light breakfast I've been eating as I hear the footsteps of an attendant coming up behind me. I exchange looks with the two other men — my subordinates — seated at the table with me, and they give me nods that are so slight as to be almost imperceptible. None of us need to exchange any more words. Both of them know what to do. And they know the price of failure.

The attendant approaches us and starts to collect the remains of our food. "I hope you gentlemen enjoyed everything?" she asks, a kind intonation to her voice. I smile up at her as I catch her eye. She's a young Swiss woman, we'd found out the night before when my men and I made our introductions, working here to save up to move to the very city we're headed: Barcelona. And she spoke to us in her native French. We'd made quite a charming impression on her — I'd made sure of that. But I feel she deserves a bit of a break from the more unruly, ritzy tourists she no doubt has to cater to on a luxury train like this.

"We couldn't have asked for better," I say, flashing a smile at her as I hand her my empty cup, "but the service is even better. Did you do something with your hair overnight?"

"Never hurts to look sharp," she says with a smile, her cheeks tinging with a little color as she gave her hair a subtle toss, pleased we'd noticed. "Never know who you'll run into, in this business."

"*Mademoiselle*, you're far too good for a gig like this," I say in a low, jokingly conspiratorial voice. "If I were you, I'd get off in Barcelona and stay there. The city's bustling with modeling agencies who'd die to get their hands on the likes of you." I am pleased to find that my French seems to be good enough that my light Georgian accent doesn't slip through too strongly. Just strongly enough to have the effect I want.

She rolls her eyes, pretending to brush off the compliment despite her smiling lips. "Sure, sure. Can I get you gentlemen anything else?"

"Actually," I say, pulling out my bag from under the table and reaching in, drawing out a bottle of champagne, "I was wondering if I could ask a small favor of you."

She tsks, but an eyebrow rises at the sight of the bottle. "You know you're not the only men on the train, I hope," she teases.

"Maybe," I say, flashing her a smile, "but if you'd be so kind as to help us bring this little surprise of ours to some friends of ours two cars ahead, we might be the only men willing to share some of it with you," I say with a wink, my dark eyes holding hers for a few moments as she bites her lip and looks around to make sure no managers are around.

"Well…" she hesitates, but my smile breaks her. "I suppose I can spare a few minutes."

"You can blame me if your manager misses you," I add as we rise to our feet, and I run a hand through my hair as the attendant leads us out the dining car and up to the private cars that have been rented out.

Such cars are usually reserved for the richest and wealthiest men and women, often tourists who are traveling Europe. Pampered types who've never known hardship in all their days, British and Americans who view the continent as their own amusement park to ride around in. The smile I wear on my face as we approach our destination is genuine. Those are precisely the types of people I'm looking forward to seeing.

"This is a private car," the attendant says, giving us a hesitant look as she reaches the door, "you're quite certain this is where your friends are seated? I…could be in a lot of trouble if I disturb the wrong group."

I reach into my pocket and pull out a hundred euro bill along with the bottle of champagne, handing both to her. "Very sure — and here's a little something for your trouble. There'll be more in it for you if you'd be so kind as to bring it in ahead of us, they don't know we're on the train with them. Tell them that Darios sends his best wishes."

She looks nervous, obviously not used to this kind of thing, and I can't blame her. I reach forward, lifting the poor girl's chin up just a bit to smile at her and watch the color come to her cheeks. "You'll do fine, *mademoiselle*. We're right behind you."

She gave an embarrassed half-laugh, running her hand through her hair before swallowing. "Of course, I'm sorry, I'm just a little flustered this morning." She clears her throat, turning and unlocking the car door and stepping inside while I step back.

Over her shoulder, I catch a glimpse of the interior. It's exactly as we expected — one large, spacious car lined with couches and a few tables, the lights low and comfortable. Along some of the couches, I see young women in incredibly expensive outfits. Designer clothing that dominated the cutting edge of the Western fashion industry, imports from Paris and Milan that many of them had probably bought during their short stays in those cities. All of them are young and beautiful, the kind of beauty only wealth affords. They're like porcelain dolls, spoiled and pampered.

And all of them are terrified.

Sure, most of the ones I can see from here do a decent job of pretending to be happy and placid as the attendant strides in nervously, but I can read the hidden emotions of other people like open books, and the thin veneer of a smile does little to hide the fear on each and every one of them.

That's because all of those women are being kidnapped and held for ransom by the other men in the car that I can't yet see.

It's an operation I know well: find spoiled young ladies traveling across Europe, abduct them, and have their terrified parents pay ludicrous amounts in ransom money. The mafia is making a killing off of this, and the men inside this car are expecting to be very rich in a week or so. I almost feel bad for spoiling their good moods. "I'll handle entry," I whisper to my men behind me, "you two back me up once the smoke is cleared."

"Excuse me, sirs and ladies," says the attendant, defaulting to heavily accented English to speak to the passengers, her tone nervous, "but I have a gift from a, um, Darios?"

"...the fuck?" I hear a male voice grunt from the car, and without wasting another moment, I draw the pistol from my jacket and step inside, aiming it at the source of the voice and pulling the trigger.

The Georgian man seated on the couch hardly has time for his eyes to widen before his brains are blown onto the window behind him.

The attendant shrieks and drops the bottle of champagne, throwing her arms up around her head, and the room explodes into chaos.

There are three more men in the room guarding the girls, and their hands are already going to their concealed weapons. The man I just killed slumps in his seat as the two women who were seated behind him cry out in terror and cringe away. I grab the attendant around the waist and sling her aside to clear the path to shoot one of the other men standing up before he can aim at me, and I dive aside as the third man points and shoots. The bullets hit the wall of the car where one of the girls had been sitting just a moment ago.

The fourth man dives for me, and I sidestep him with ease, but he pulls a knife on me, and I'm forced to engage. His movements are quick and precise, but I get a hold of his wrist before he can land a strike, and I twist him around. I know the third gunman is trying to aim a shot at me, so I don't stop moving, flowing around him like water and trying to keep my man blocking my line of sight.

Finally, I move out of my living cover long enough for the gunman to think he has a shot, but I twist the knife-fighter around by the wrist, and I hear a gunshot go off just as I pull him in front of me, and I hear him grunt as his own ally's bullet hits his heart, and he slumps to the ground just as I level my gun at the shooter.

In a matter of seconds, three men have been killed, and most of the already terrified girls in the car are taking what cover they can under the tables, watching the fight with wide eyes. The attendant just laid down flat, covering her head with her hands among the broken glass.

And the man I see looking down the barrel of my gun makes me want to risk pulling the trigger right here and now.

"Darios Esadze," he says, narrowing his eyes at me and smiling as I clench my jaw. "I was wondering whether I'd ever see you again, my old friend."

"Luka," I say back, evenly. "It *has* been a while. If I'd have seen you any other time after the war, you'd be a dead man, you fucking traitor." Luka's distinctive, curly red hair that spills down his shoulders could be spotted a mile away. It accents his cruel face fittingly. What felt like a lifetime ago, he fought by my side against the Russians in the fallout of the Ossetian uprising. "I'm surprised the Russians didn't kill you after you sold out to them."

"The lives of your comrades was enough for them," he taunts, trying to egg me on into a fight. Before I can reply, there's a gunshot from the door of the car, and Luka cries out in pain, his left hand blown clean off by the shot of one of my subordinates as the two of them stride in, training pistols on him.

A smile crosses my face as I step forward to the bleeding man, grabbing him by the collar and lifting him into the air with one hand as he cradles the stump at his wrist, his gun forgotten on the floor. He looks up at me, pain on his face through his sneer. "You want your revenge, then?" he spits, "Take it, you greedy bastard!"

"No," I say, my voice dripping with contempt, "no, you'll live a little longer." I stride over to the other side of the car, opening the door to the outdoors that's rushing by us rapidly, wind whipping inside as Luka winces in pain. "You're going to take that bloody stump of yours and bring it to your superiors as a message: you're not running this operation anymore."

Before he has a chance to speak, I toss him out the door, watching him hit the ground with a thump before the train flies by, leaving him far, far behind in a matter of moments. I wonder if he'll survive the hobble to the nearest hospital. It matters little — the Georgian mafia will have little interest in keeping him around after news of this failure reaches them.

I shut the door and turn around, surveying the damage. My men start to put their guns away, looking to me for orders as a couple of the women start to peek out of their hiding spots, wide-eyed and staring at me in absolute awe. The attendant is even starting to get to her feet carefully, as amazed as I am that she's unharmed.

With a cry of delight, one of the women in a skirt worth more than the guns we're carrying steps forward to me with shining eyes, a broad smile on her face. "Oh my god," she gasps, "oh my god, thank you! They said they were going to take us for ransom, you saved our lives!"

She throws her arms around me, and I chuckle as I pat her on the back, then reach down and take her by the chin, lifting it slowly to look me in the eyes. As she looks into them, her smile starts to fade.

"You poor, spoiled girl," I chide, my tone genuinely amused as I twirl some of her hair around my finger, and my men start to move about the room and direct the other confused women back into their seats. "I'm afraid this isn't a rescue. I'm taking this operation over."

I hear the attendant behind me inching towards the car door, and without looking away from the teary-eyed girl in front of me, I point my gun at the attendant and hear her freeze.

"You've been a gem, *mademoiselle*," I say sincerely. "Now take a seat with the others. I think a lovely girl like you will fetch a fair ransom as well."

Today is the day my life is going to change.

I knew it from the second I woke up this morning and realized what I have to do. Instead of trailing along after my parents down the boring, historical streets of Europe while they drone on and on about what battles were fought where and badger me about what I'm going to major in at college, I'm going to have my own little trip.

Don't get me wrong. I'm still going to Europe. And I'm still going to meet up with my parents in Switzerland so they can share historical anecdotes and lecture me about responsibility, or whatever they have planned. But first, I'm going to make this weekend one heck of a rendezvous.

I graduated high school just a few days ago, and I just turned eighteen a month before that, so I'm at a place in life where I should probably be starting to figure things out. I should have a plan by now, right? I should know where I'm headed and why.

I should know who I am.

But if my eighteen years on this planet have taught me anything at all, it's that sometimes who you really are isn't what the world actually wants from you. In fact, it's been my experience that good things only happen when I pretend to be someone I'm not — until enough time has passed that who I have to be turned into who I've become.

If that makes any sense.

Anyway, the point is, sometimes you have to fake it 'til you make it. And that's what I've been doing for the past six years — faking it. And now I'm so good at being this version of Delaney Underwood that nobody even remembers the way I used to be, back before I woke up and realized I would never succeed until I became someone else entirely. It's all a role, something my parents pushed on me until I just couldn't resist any longer.

I've been playing this part for so long now that *I* can scarcely remember what I used to be like.

I sit up in bed and stretch, a yawn escaping my mouth as I swing my legs over the side of my plush, four-poster bed and trudge across the room to sit in front of my vanity mirror. I reach over and pull the jeweled cord of a designer lamp to my left, casting a pillar of bright white light across my face. I survey my face critically in the mirror, scanning for imperfections, for a flaw in the armor I must wear every day.

I smile to myself, realizing with a sigh of relief that there are no blemishes, no problems at all with the reflection in the mirror. I do this every morning, blinking blearily into my mirror with a sense of creeping worry, as though I might one day see some hideous, unfamiliar face staring back at me instead of my own. Sometimes it feels like I'm living under some magic spell, and at any moment the rug could be pulled out from underneath me. My life is good — really, really good — and I know I should be grateful, but when you get used to living a certain way, it just becomes your new normal.

Even if this wasn't who I used to be… it's me *now*.

I bat my wide, china-blue eyes and give myself a coquettish smile, my dimples appearing identically in each smooth cheek. There is a light smattering of freckles across my straight button nose, and my lips are full and pouty. People tell me I'm pretty; in fact, my entire existence is predicated on that fact thanks to my parents. What I am, the way I live my life, it all depends on my looks. And I've worked hard to get to this point.

I pick up a brush and sweep my long, gently curling champagne-blonde hair over one shoulder and begin to tame the snarls created during my night of tossing and turning. During the day, nobody can possibly see through the opaque shield of cool, unapproachable beauty I've built around myself. But at night, when I'm left all alone with my thoughts… that's when my old weaknesses and insecurities start to rear their ugly heads. I tend to have nightmares a lot. Sometimes I'm walking through the halls of my high school naked, my classmates jeering and laughing uproariously at me. Sometimes I'm just falling, falling, falling into an empty abyss. I wake up in a cold sweat, feeling lonely and afraid.

But if having bad dreams every other night is the price I have to pay for excellence in my waking hours, then so be it, my parents would say. I'll take whatever I can get.

Smoothing my hair down so that it falls in luxurious waves around my shoulders, I walk over to my dresser and pull out a flowy white-and-blue striped tank top, pair it with a pair of denim shorts, and then make my way into my spacious en suite bathroom to wash my face and put on makeup. I enjoy the ritual of putting on makeup. It's like putting on a mask and reinventing myself. It's a fun way to express myself and enhance my looks. With everyone believing in the power of Photoshop, and the stunning models plastered everywhere, the expectations on women keep getting higher, and I aim to keep up.

I apply a cursory layer of mascara, a sheer BB cream to my face, and dab some rosy-tinted gloss onto my lips. Blowing a kiss into the mirror, I decide I look good enough to venture out into the world.

It's summertime, and I have a plan to set in motion.

I STROLL down the hallway of the huge, palatial estate I live in with my parents, basking in the light streaming in through the floor-to-ceiling windows. There are birds singing gleefully outside, and not a cloud in the sky. The perfect day.

When I walk into the kitchen, I am greeted by the welcoming scent of fresh coffee brewing. I pour myself a mug, stir in some non-fat creamer, and grab a croissant from the covered dish on the counter before walking out onto the back pavilion. Here in Savannah, Georgia, it's not unusual to see houses left over from the days of plantations. Ours is one such house, a massive, white colonial-style estate with a full front porch and a few acres of lush green land-scaping. There's an in ground pool and gazebo in the backyard, and the latter of which is my favorite place to sit and enjoy the morning.

I settle down onto the cushioned swing seat under the gazebo, just out of the sun's harsh rays but still open to the fresh, balmy air. Butterflies and dragonflies buzz and flutter lazily around the yard, alighting on the blooms of my mother's rose garden. There is the pervasive smell of jasmine and hibiscus in the air, and I close my eyes, inhaling deeply. There's no denying the fact that being outside, surrounded by nature, is one of my most cherished activities, despite my high-maintenance persona. Sometimes when the elaborate dog-and-pony show of my life gets to be too much, and I just want to shed the layers of make believe and feel authentic for once, I just step outside and walk among the immaculately-maintained trees, bushes, and flowers of my backyard. It's refreshing to know that nature doesn't care about what I pretend to be or what I used to be — it simply exists. The natural world is ever-changing, yet comfortingly constant.

Unlike my world.

As I sip my coffee and nibble my croissant, I reflect on what all it has taken for me to make this total transformation. Out of the corner of my eye, I spot a little cocoon dangling from the wooden awning of the gazebo. I give it a sympathetic smile, thinking, *I know how you feel.*

For the first twelve years of my life, I was just a little caterpillar. Chubby, innocent, unaware of the world around me. I lived in my own little universe, my nose constantly buried in the pages of some fantasy novel. I wore thick glasses and paid very little attention to my looks, despite my beauty queen mother's attempts to make me more attractive. As a child, I simply didn't care what I looked like. I was a smart kid, always devouring new information, and I wasn't afraid to show off my knowledge and wits. I was always the first one to raise my hand in class, always the top student. And I was content with that… until puberty started to kick in.

Seventh grade. That was my turning point.

When I was twelve years old, I looked across the classroom and my eyes fell on the cutest boy I had ever seen: Brandon Grier. He had cropped brown hair and blue eyes and I thought he looked just like the princes in my fantasy books. I spent the entire seventh grade year casting sidelong glances at him, dreaming that he would one day notice me. At that point, I was naive and childish enough to think that I was good enough for a guy like him. I didn't know that my unkempt hair, nerdy interests, and chunky glasses would disqualify me as "his kind of girl." At the end of the year, on the last day of school, I finally plucked up the courage to talk to him.

It went a little something like this…

"Hi, Brandon! Now that it's summer, I was wondering if maybe you might want to come over and play with my new microscope set sometime?" I asked, full of guileless optimism.

"Um, no. Because I'm not a loser," my prince charming snorted cruelly.

Cue the derisive laughter of my entire seventh

grade class as I rushed out of the room to go cry in the bathroom for an hour until our housekeeper — who doubled as a chef and a nanny — came to pick me up from school.

I shudder to think about that horrible day. It was the first time reality had stepped in and slapped me across the face, forcing me to really think about my life in a critical way. Up until then, I had been content to live in my fantasy books and imagine a world that suited me better. But after Brandon unceremoniously trampled my heart, it became clear to me that if I wanted to survive in *this* world, I needed to change myself.

And so I did. I spent that whole summer poring over magazines, scouring the internet for Cosmo tips on how to become pretty and desirable — which was, admittedly, an unhealthy obsession for a twelve year old to indulge in. But my father has always been endlessly supportive of anything and everything I want to do, and my mother was overjoyed at the opportunity to finally mold me into the picture-perfect princess she always wanted.

So with a combination of my daddy's money and my mom's tutelage, I entered the cocoon and emerged in my thirteenth year as a much smoother, sleeker version of my former self. Over the course of grade eight, I continued to bolster my skills at dressing and preening myself, and then over the summer before I started high school, I went away to a finishing school crash course my mother had been pushing for years.

When I stepped into the halls of my high school on the first day of freshman year, I looked like a totally different girl. I transformed from a slightly chubby, nerdy little outcast into the very definition of the It Girl. It didn't take long for everyone to notice. For the first time in my life, boys were interested in me. Girls were jealous of me. People hung on my every word and competed for my attention. Brandon Grier asked me out, and I said yes. He didn't seem to remember the time I regretfully approached him in seventh grade, and I didn't remind him. That was part of my past, and it didn't jive with the new, improved Delaney Underwood.

She didn't hold on to regrets. It was all about the future, and the stepping stones I needed to walk on to become the person my parents wanted me to be. Even though my dad had always been supportive, I couldn't help but notice his relief at my more *traditional* interests. In fact, no matter who I talked to, they seemed to expect me to be the butterfly I became.

It was an intoxicating rush.

And I have been riding that high for years.

Of course, there is a downside to shedding your old self — sometimes, you lose even the parts of you that you kind of liked to begin with. For instance, nowadays I don't have the same thirst for knowledge I once had. In fact, to keep in line with my super-cool ice queen persona, I have had to feign nonchalance for so long that I hardly feel much of anything anymore. Instead of being top of the class, I simply skate by with passing grades. For a while, I was the head cheerleader, and I was pretty damn good. But when talent scouts started hounding me, I quit the squad, not wanting to commit myself to anything too lofty.

My whole identity is based on being too cool for… well, anything.

And just because I play the role of a vapid blonde doesn't mean I'm not still smart — I just use my wits in a different way. Instead of studying physics, I study people. I am a master manipulator, especially when it comes to men, of all ages. All it takes is a sweet, disarming smile or the flip of my shiny blonde hair and I can render a man harmless.

My dad is no different. He's too busy with his demanding job to really question anything I do, and he spoils me endlessly. My mom is a little better at seeing through my innocent act, but she's too consumed with her own attempts to maintain the beauty of her youth to really pay much attention to me. She spends most of her time flitting between the tanning salon, the dermatologist, the hair salon, department stores, the nail salon, and martinis with the girls.

Of course, sometimes my charm backfires. Brandon, my now ex-boyfriend, is still devoted to me — almost to the point of being a stalker. I broke up with him on the day of graduation. I never forgot that he broke my heart, even if I let him believe I was in love.

But he still calls and texts me constantly, acting like we're still together, like he just refuses to accept that I don't want to be with him anymore. I got tired of his begging for me to give him my virginity, to commit to him, to give in to a life of being his trophy girlfriend and inevitably his trophy wife.

Here's the thing: I may look the part, and for all the world I may act the part, but I know where to draw my limits. I'm nobody's little plaything. I don't know where I'm going from here, but I know I don't want to end up wasting away polishing china sets and waiting for my husband to come home and pay attention to me. I'm just not that girl.

I look at some of the brazen little sparrows, chirping around the little feed box that hangs in the corner of the gazebo, and hear their little sister chirp weakly. She'd fallen from their nest a couple weeks ago, and I really thought she was going to die. The mother had abandoned her, so I took her into a tiny cage, slowly trying to nurse her back to health.

It really wasn't easy, and my friends would all have abandoned me if they realized I was grinding up earthworms to feed her every day, but I'm really happy she seems to be doing better. I toss the rest of my croissant to her brothers as I lean down and look in on her cage.

Putting my finger through the bars, she quickly lands on it, peeping at me urgently. I can't help but laugh as I reach for the little bug catcher I keep near her cage, and pull out a small worm. She's gotten old enough that she's able to do it herself now, and when I place it in the cage, she ravenously eats it.

I'm filled with mixed feelings at her healing. Part of me is proud that I managed to nurse her back to health, but a bigger part of me is sad, because I know I'm going to have to let her go before my big plan. She's trapped in a tiny cage, never able to soar in the skies and stretch her wings.

I feel a lot like her, honestly, so maybe setting her free will be cathartic.

"Maybe both of us will finally feel free, sweet bird," I say wistfully. Draining the rest of my coffee in one gulp, I stand up and head back inside to confront my parents with the plan I concocted last night.

Well, at least the plan they'll *think* I have.

My parents are lounging in the breakfast nook while our housekeeper, Marie, tidies up in the kitchen. I step into the room and clear my throat. My dad looks up from the newspaper in his hands and my mom merely flutters her fingers at me in a kind of girlish greeting, not even tearing her eyes away from the iPad in her lap. I can tell from the look on her face that she's online shopping. As usual.

"Good morning, sweetheart," my dad says, smiling warmly at the sight of me.

"Hi, Daddy," I reply sweetly, walking over to hug him and perch on the arm of his chair.

"Are you all packed for the flight out tomorrow morning?" he asks, folding the newspaper and setting it aside. Here it was. Time to launch *Operation Freedom Weekend*.

I bite my lip and tilt my head to one side, making myself look concerned. "Actually, I wanted to talk to you about that."

"Oh? What's wrong, Laney?" he questions, his thick brows furrowing. I take a deep breath and tuck my hair back behind my ear.

"Well, you see, there's this college counselor coming into town to take interviews with potential students and I really want to go meet with her. I know I have to start really taking charge of my future and I don't want to miss this opportunity. And… the only time she's available to meet with me is this weekend," I explain, staring downward sadly.

"You're going to meet with a college counselor on a Saturday?" my mom pipes up, giving me a slightly suspicious look. Damn it. She's always quick to point out the flaws in my plan. Luckily, my dad is the one who makes the decisions around here, and I've got him wrapped around my little finger.

"Well, maybe we can just postpone the trip for a few days," he suggests. "I wouldn't want to leave you here alone while your mother and I go gallivanting off to Europe."

"Oh, no! You two should go ahead and I will meet you in Switzerland. Don't postpone your trip because of me," I counter quickly, wanting to stick to my own plan. The whole point is for them to go on without me.

"Well, I would just feel so awful making you fly over there all by yourself, sweetheart. It's just not safe for such a sweet girl to travel alone," Daddy says, scratching at his chin thoughtfully. My mom is casting puppy dog eyes at him, clearly not wanting to postpone their trip, either. Seeing this, I jump at the chance to work another angle.

"I'm eighteen years old, Daddy! I can handle it. Besides, you and Mom never get to have any time to yourselves. Wouldn't it be nice to have a whole romantic weekend in Europe before I show up?" I add, shrugging. My parents exchange knowing glances and I have to resist the urge to shudder. Ew.

"I suppose that might be nice," my dad says, starting to warm up to my idea. "But the thought of my little girl traveling so far by herself still worries me. What if I give you my credit card and you buy flights for you and a friend? Maybe Caitlin? I'm sure her parents wouldn't mind if she took a little trip to Europe. She can fly over with you to meet us, spend a few days, and then fly back home."

I light up with excitement. This is turning out even better than I'd hoped!

"Oh my goodness. That would be perfect! What a good idea," I say excitedly, throwing my arms around him. He chuckles and pats me on the back fondly.

"Anything for my little angel," he replies. "Especially if this is something good for your future. Picking a college is very important. I know you're still not sure which school you want to go to, and I think meeting with a counselor will really..."

I pretend to listen dutifully as my dad goes on and on about the importance of going to the right school and getting the right degree. I've heard it all a million times before. He wants me to go to an Ivy League — despite my grades — and part of me wants that to. The part of me I keep locked up, deep inside and hidden away. Once he gets a call from the office, he cuts the lecture short and heads off to work. It's not long before my mom flounces out to meet her friends for a drink and a manicure, leaving me home alone.

Grinning victoriously to myself, I send a group text to my three closest friends, Caitlin, Lyssa, and Megan, and fill them in on the details. There is no interview with a college counselor. Instead, the four of us are all going to buy flights to Barcelona tomorrow afternoon on my daddy's credit card, after my parents leave. My girls and I are going to have one hell of a weekend in Spain — responsibilities be damned.

Nothing can go wrong.

"¡*Cuatro cervezas, por favor!*" chirps my friend Lyssa, reclining next to me as she bats her eyelashes up at the handsome waiter. My three closest friends and I are all lounging poolside at a resort in Barcelona, Spain, and we look fantastic. Lyssa, with her nut-brown skin and long black braids; Caitlin, with her sleek, shoulder-length chocolate-colored hair and flirtatious eyes; Megan, with her russet curls and milky-white skin; and me.

I'm wearing a new bathing suit I bought just last week in preparation for this secret trip. My full, perky breasts are barely covered by the lilac-colored bikini top and my flat stomach and toned thighs are out on display. I've got a giant white floppy sun hat shading my face so I don't burn, and I've almost completely downed my first margarita of the day.

"Could I get mine with a lime wedge, please?"

Megan whispers, biting her lip.

"*Con un limón, también,*" Lyssa adds flippantly. The waiter nods and walks back up to the little bar under the gazebo. My friend looks at me and winks. "Lucky for y'all, I actually paid attention in Spanish class instead of just passing notes the whole time."

"Oh, whatever. You only paid attention because you thought Señor Martinez was hot," Caitlin breaks in, laughing.

"Ugh, I forgot about that! So gross, Lyssa," Megan giggles. "He was like a million years old, wasn't he?"

"No! He's only like thirty or something," Lyssa says defensively, her cheeks flushing with embarrassment even as she grins.

"Okay, okay, leave her alone!" I chide the other two. "We're all adults here, alright? If Lyssa wants to lust after some gross old guy, that's her prerogative."

"Hey!" she laughs, swatting at me playfully.

The waiter returns with our beers and I tell him to put it all on my tab. "Daddy's credit card is getting a nice work out here," I comment nonchalantly, sipping my beer.

"Isn't he gonna be mad when he sees the bank statements?" Caitlin asks.

I wave my hand dismissively. "Nah. Well, maybe. But either way, he never stays mad at me for long. And it's easier to ask for forgiveness than permission."

"That's true," Megan agrees.

"Besides, it's not like I bought four plane tickets. Just the two he told me to buy, for me and Caitlin," I reply, shrugging. Luckily, Megan and Lyssa both also have wealthy parents who are too tied up in their own business to really care all that much about what their daughters get up to when they're not looking. Caitlin's parents are a little stricter, but they also trust me implicitly. It's a skill I've honed over time — I can charm the pants off of anyone's parents. All I have to do is pull the same act I do with my own dad, and people are falling over themselves to please me. I'm very good at convincing people I can be trusted — even if that's a mistake.

I should not be trusted.

But nobody ever realizes that until it's too late.

As we're reclining on our lounge chairs, sunning ourselves and chatting mindlessly, an exceptionally handsome guy saunters up to us, giving us an approving smirk and a once-over. I can tell instantly that he likes what he sees. And the feeling is mutual.

"*Buenos dias, bellas,*" he greets us in Spanish, stopping in front of us with his hands on his hips.

"*Hola,*" Lyssa breathes, her brown eyes wide with awe at this delicious hunk of man standing before us. I almost want to reach over and nudge her out of it. My friends aren't quite as good at playing the ice queen as I am. Lyssa is the smart, athletic one, Megan is the sweet one, and Caitlin is the fire to my ice.

Caitlin immediately sits up and fixes the guy with a smoldering gaze. She's the most forward and aggressive of the group, for certain, and she will flirt with anything that moves. Biting her lip coyly, she replies in flawed Spanish, "Hey handsome, what's up?"

I can tell by the bewildered look on her face, Lyssa is blindsided to find out that she's not the only one who knows a fair smattering of Spanish. I have to stifle a laugh. This is so typical. Of course Caitlin only puts her skills to use when there's a hot piece of ass at stake.

He asks us where we're from, and I quickly tell him that we're from the United States. The guy's face lights up, both in response to my answer and to the fact that I am addressing him now.

"Ah, I speak English," he replies with a grin. "You girls are beautiful. Welcome to Barcelona. I hope you're having a good time here."

"We are now," I answer, lifting one eyebrow and blessing him with a faint smile.

"I was wondering, would you all like to go to a rooftop party tonight?" the guy asks.

"Oh my god, yes!" Megan bursts out. I give her a silencing glance.

"What time?" Caitlin pipes up.

"Fiesta starts around ten. If you give me your number I'll text you the address," he says, giving me a wink and grin. *Muy suave,* I think to myself.

"You got it," I reply, taking a pen out of my purse and then standing up to write my number on the guy's hand. His eyes never leave my face. When I'm done, I look up to meet his gaze and he smiles broadly.

"Excellent. See you tonight, chicas," he says. "I'm Raúl, by the way."

"Delaney," I answer, giving him a little wave as he swaggers away, glancing back at me over his shoulder as he disappears into the crowd by the bar.

Spinning around, I excitedly gesture for the girls to get up.

"Finish your drinks, ladies. Sunbathing time is over. We got a party tonight! Looks like we have some shopping to do!" I announce brightly. The four of us chug our drinks, making sour faces in the process, then laughing at each other's expression. After I walk over to the bar to pay the tab, we pack up our stuff and head up to the hotel suite to change into sundresses and hit the town for some retail therapy.

WE SPEND the next several hours traipsing down the beautiful, colorful streets of Barcelona, winding in and out of designer shops and vintage stores in search of the perfect ensembles for an evening out. With each of our credit cards in hand, we spare no expense, too brazen and excited to shy away from even the steepest price tags. The four of us are all accustomed to an exceptionally high standard of living back in Savannah, and it only seems fair that we follow that same path when overseas.

With her tall, athletic frame, Lyssa decides on a flowy white dress to contrast attractively with her dark skin, accented with a thin, gold-chain necklace. She's the girl who has it all: wealth, intellect, and confidence. She's the girl I wanted to be, but never could, and I can't help but feel a pang of jealousy as she struts around in her outfit.

Megan picks out a romantic pale blue frock and a pair of shiny white-gold earrings for the night.

"Caitlin, what are you thinking?" I ask, idly shuffling through a rack of glittery dresses which are a little too nightclubby for my taste. She holds up a sparkling, skin-tight gold mini-dress and black stiletto heels, raising her eyebrows suggestively.

"Oh my god, that would look incredible on you," Megan gasps, her eyes wide.

"It's a little, um, flashy. Don't you think?" Lyssa comments, shaking her head.

"Well, duh. I'm not trying to blend in here, Lyssa. I want to stand out. I want every one of those sexy Spanish guys to check me out. Your girl's gettin' laid tonight, whatever it takes," Caitlin laughs. I give her a nod of approval.

"Looks good to me! You slut," I add fondly.

"Thanks," she replies, giggling as she sashays back to the fitting rooms.

"She's going to look like my volleyball trophy in that gold dress," Lyssa remarks, with a surprising dose of cattiness.

"Oh, let her do her thing," I scold her. "We're here to have fun, not police each other's outfits. If you wanna play the judge, you can help me out. I still don't know what to wear."

Lyssa and Megan both light up at the chance to dress me. With my soft curves and nearly ethereal coloring, my friends are always excited to help me pick out clothes. I'm sure a lot of that has to do with the fact that I have subtly cultivated a sense of dominance over them. All three of my best friends are constantly vying for my attention in one way or another. In return, I look out for them and help them achieve the popularity they want. It's a mutually-beneficial relationship.

The girls all pitch in to help me find the perfect outfit, and we decide on a classic form-fitting black dress that falls to about mid-thigh, with a deep scoop neck that shows off an abundance of cleavage.

With our purchases in hand, we go out for a victorious pre-party dinner at a swanky restaurant around the corner from our resort hotel. We order a round of delicious tapas, along with a pitcher of sangria to share. Laughing and chatting excitedly about the night ahead, two hours pass quickly and before we know it, it's time for us to rush up to the suite and get changed for the night that will undoubtedly stand out in our memories for years to come.

Finally, the hour has arrived.

Adorned in our brand-new outfits, the four of us pile into a cab and ride to the address Raúl texted to me. The moon is well into her descent up into the velvety black sky above us and the four of us are awestruck by the romantic lighting and feel the streets in this part of town. We can hear the sounds of muffled music from far above, a party clearly going on atop the roof of this building. Exchanging excited grins, we all link arms and rush up the steps to the front entrance. A man with a thick beard and a halfway-unbuttoned shirt lets us in after I tell him Raúl sent us.

"Elevator straight back. Go to rooftop," he remarks in a rather bored voice.

"*Gracias*," Lyssa quips, nodding at him as we pass through.

"This is amazing," Megan gushes.

"Everyone remain calm," Caitlin hisses, but there's a delighted grin on her face. We pile into the elevator and ride it all the way to the top, the pounding bass of the music getting louder and louder as we ascend. When the doors open, we are greeted by an inundation of music, with a group of nine or ten guys all drinking and laughing together.

When we walk out of the elevator, all heads turn, all eyes focusing on us.

For a moment, an uncharacteristic shock of panic floods my system. But when the guys gesture for us to come on over, my nervousness fades. I remind myself that even though this may be a foreign country, boys are the same everywhere you go. And if there's one thing I can definitely handle, it's a group of horny boys.

Especially when the alcohol is flowing freely.

It's not long before everyone is dancing to the pumping music, drinks in hand. It strikes me as a little odd that we are some of the only girls here, but when I note this to Caitlin, she quickly replies in an undertone, "That's exactly the kind of ratio I like!"

I can't exactly argue with her, seeing as every single man on this rooftop is blindingly handsome and a fantastic dancer. But they're all fairly pedestrian in comparison to the guy standing in the corner, looking out over the city. Something about him draws me closer, makes me want to see him more clearly. But he's spent most of the evening so far being standoffish, like he's too good for this, too good for us.

But nobody is too good for me.

So once I've downed my third shot of rum, I saunter over to him, already assuming my usual wide-eyed ingénue persona. Generally, this is one of my most successful acts. Boys can never resist a girl they think they can dominate, a girl who looks like she needs to be corrupted.

Little do they know, I'm the one pulling their strings.

"*Hola,*" I say sweetly, taking a spot beside him, leaning on the railing. "What are you doing way over here?"

The guy hesitates before looking down at me, as though he can't be bothered. But I catch the little flicker in his eyes when he does meet my gaze. He's interested, even if he doesn't want to show it.

"I doubt that's any of your business," the guy answers coolly, and the accent peppering his words isn't Spanish, but I can't quite place it. I'm a little taken aback by his words and the casual dismissal.

"Oh, I didn't mean to bother you," I reply, batting my eyelashes and biting my lip apologetically. "You just looked lonely."

"And you're just the girl to change my mood, are you?" he says, turning to face me with a hint of a challenge in his expression. "You think just because you're a pretty little thing, I'm just going to fall all over you, yes?"

I'm stunned, the words falling dead in my throat.

Then, the guy gives me a roguish, charming grin and holds out his hand for me to shake.

"Darios. And you are?"

"Delaney," I answer, shaking his hand.

"You look like you could use another drink," he says. "What's your poison, *genatsvale?*"

"I've been doing rum shots," I answer. He scoffs.

"Not anymore," Darios says, wrapping an arm around my shoulders and guiding me toward the little makeshift bar area to pour me a drink, the contents of which I don't even recognize. But when I sip it, I'm immediately shocked by a wave of warmth through my body.

"What is this?" I ask innocently. But he merely gives me a bemused smirk and pulls me onto the dance floor, his hands sliding down to my waist. I never let anyone manhandle me quite like this — usually I need to be in control. But something about this guy has knocked me off-kilter. Something about his quietly powerful presence, his piercing dark eyes and sharp, handsome face… he looks like trouble, and I'm ready to give into it. For once.

As we move together to the music, he pulls me closer, his muscular body sliding against mine while he leans down to gently brush his lips along the shell of my ear. A shiver travels down my spine and he laughs quietly, cruelly, like he knows exactly what he's doing to me.

Over the course of the night we dance this way, our bodies moving together in the balmy summer night, neither of us talking very much at all. We don't need words. And I realized quickly that this guy isn't like the boys back home. He's older, more sophisticated… darker. He can't be so easily manipulated by the flutter of my lashes or the sweetness of my voice. It's admittedly a little frightening to think that I'm not the one with the upper hand, but at the same time, I can't deny how exhilarating it feels to finally meet someone who challenges me.

And he makes me feel things I've never felt before.

My body is starting to tingle and feel weak, exhausted by the combination of jet lag, a busy day, and hours of dancing and drinking. I surrender control, letting Darios hold me up, his artful hands deftly guiding me around the dancefloor, gripping my waist and my hips with a sense of control I've never allowed anyone to hold over me.

By the time the party is beginning to wind down, I'm more than ready to give up that most precious gift that I've been keeping secret and safe for years: my virginity. For even though I dated Brandon for years, and even though he pressured me incessantly to give it up, I never let him convince me. I've guarded my heart and my body obsessively all this time, but now… I want to let it go. It just feels right. And I know without a doubt that Darios is worthy.

The music fades away and the men start packing up. Darios whispers in my ear, "You girls wait here while we take everything downstairs. Give us a few minutes and then come down. We'll get the cars ready to go."

I can only nod, my mind fuzzy with alcohol and desire.

My friends look to be in similar states of mind, all of them bleary-eyed but excited. Megan trudges over and rests her head on my shoulder. "This is the best night ever," she says.

"I think I might sleep with that guy I was dancing with," Lyssa hisses.

"We're all getting laid tonight," Caitlin remarks devilishly.

Even me, I think to myself. After a few minutes, we head downstairs, all of us exhausted but spurred on by adrenaline and awe. When the elevator doors open and we step out into the quiet, dark lobby, nobody is in sight. For a moment, I wonder sadly if maybe the guys ditched us, after all.

But then there's a chorus of ominous clicks, a glint of light hitting metal in a complete circle around the four of us. "What the hell?" I whisper, looking around in confusion.

From the darkness, all the men step forward holding guns, which are held straight out, aimed directly at the four of us. Darios walks a few steps closer until he stands directly in front of me. Giving me a terrifyingly handsome smile, he says, "We had a really good time with you girls tonight, but the party doesn't have to end yet. In fact, we're just going to switch venues. Follow us out, be quiet, behave your-selves, and nobody has to get hurt. Yet."

The next few minutes go like clockwork, exactly as we've done our business many a time before this group. A couple of the girls ask if this is some kind of joke, it isn't funny anymore, and one of them offers some paltry bit of money or jewelry to convince us to let them go as we herd them towards the vans we have parked around the corner.

"Shut *up*, Megan," snaps Caitlin as her ditzy friend tries to offer one of my men her necklace.

"No, you don't get it!" the bottle-blonde stammers, "th-this is Florentine gold, it's probably worth more than your whole outfit, y'know? I-I'm sure you could buy whatever you wanted with it, like a ticket out of here or something!"

"Hush, girl," growls the man who'd been flirting with her all night, luring her into the trap we'd perfected laying for these spoiled Western girls. When we reach the vans, our guns concealed under our jackets, I line the girls up to face the vehicle.

"Arms up, ladies," I order, and they exchange nervous glances with one another before slowly putting their arms up. I give a nod to one of my men, who steps forward to start patting the girls down. It's more and more likely that they carry concealed weapons or pepper spray these days, so it's better to be safe. As he goes to work, I take a moment to evaluate our catches of the night as I cross my arms, striding behind them thoughtfully, looming over the whole scene.

I take it upon myself to remember the names of each one. That's why we don't take them right away. We get to know them first, intimately, disarm them and find out their personalities and weaknesses. Toying with them demands a level of familiarity, so it's much easier to deal with them if I know a little about them, and my perceptiveness has never failed me. And as we marched the ladies to the van, my men gave me their reports on each of them. Caitlin is a strong-willed girl, just another spoiled daughter of some tycoon fighting off rivals. She whispers to my man as he pats her down, and he ignores her, finding the can of mace in her purse and stowing it. She might make a show of being hard to deal with, but she'll break soon enough.

Lyssa is the dark-skinned girl, and she seems

more level-headed than some of the others. She rides the coattails of her parents' wealth like all the rest, but I have a feeling that the longer she stays in our possession, the fiercer her resistance will grow. As she's patted down, she's very still, but I can see the tension in her, suppressing her fear. We might have to be careful with that one if her parents drag their feet.

Caitlin is the brunette, the one who still hasn't understood the gravity of the situation. She seems agitated more than afraid, as if she's never come up against a problem that she couldn't solve outright. She's working the entire situation as if it's a puzzle to solve.

Megan was a delight for her seducer to toy with. She seems to have let her wits fall to the wayside in the daze of wealth she grew up around, because her mannerisms betray an airheadedness that makes her beautifully easy to manipulate. There are tears in her eyes as my man searches her. Still, we should ransom her off first. The parents of such a girl are more likely to jump at the chance of getting their precious ditz out of danger.

Then there's my prey. Delaney. As the guard steps forward to inspect her, I wave him off, stepping forward myself. There's something about this one that I can't quite place, but it sets her apart from the rest. She's been very still, and after a moment, I realize she's been taking in everything around her —

listening to our voices, stealing as many glances at our faces as she can. I feel a smile spreading across my face as I reach out and set my hands on her shoulders, squeezing her narrow frame gently as I start to run my hands down her sides, then to her hips. She's at least observant, I'll give her that. I let her blonde hair run through my fingers like strands of sunlight, twirling a lock around my finger.

"What the hell could I possibly have in there?" she snaps, and I raise my eyebrows. Amusing little show of defiance. This one is more interesting than I thought. I give a smile as I take a handful of her hair a little more firmly, tugging it and forcing her to tilt her head back as I lean in to her.

"My attention," I reply in a low tone, and I can almost feel the shiver of excitement that runs up her back. I had to admit, this one had my attention from the moment I'd laid eyes on her. She was nearly a full foot shorter than me, with a narrow frame and crystal-blue eyes, the likes of which I'd never seen before in my travels. And those ruby-red lips of hers could drive a man wild. I wonder how many boys she'd captivated with that round face of hers, the slight upturn of her nose, and those soft cheeks. It was no wonder she was the leader of this little group.

"You can have all our money," she says, "even the credit cards, I swear we won't call and cancel them. You can get whatever you want." The men let out a light chuckle behind me, but I turn Delaney around, letting her look into my endless dark eyes that captivated her so easily just a few minutes ago, a smile on my face.

"Sweet girl," I say, crooking my finger and lifting her chin to raise her eyes to mine, "I think you've misunderstood what this is. But you're right about one thing," I say as I take out a long strip of black fabric from my pocket, extending it between my hands. I watch her eyes widen as I start to raise it to cover her vision. "I *will* get whatever I want from you."

Moments later, my men have done the same with the other girls, blindfolding their eyes and binding their hands behind them before we lead them into the back of the vans. We split the girls up, taking Delaney and Megan in one car, while Lyssa and Caitlin ride in the other. In each van, two men sit in the back with the girls to make sure they're well-guarded. After the driver is seated in the front, I get in the back, sliding in close beside Delaney.

"Get comfortable," I whisper to her, my voice a low growl, "we have a long ride ahead of us."

She says nothing. I smile. I'm going to enjoy this little brat.

"I-I THINK my uncle has a summer house around Seville," I hear Megan speak up in her pathetic squeak for about the third or fourth time during the trip. "You can have that! I promise it's worth a lot!"

"I don't think they're interested, Megan," Delaney says, and I can feel her tense a little against me. Her dim friend has been vocal the whole ride, trying to bargain for her freedom, while Delaney has been far more guarded. My presence next to her has helped guarantee that. While Megan is sitting alone, her guard watching her from the other side of the van, I hold Delaney's restraints myself, a thumb hooked within them. As she speaks, I give her a tug, smiling at how easily I can control her. When she feels me tug, she tests her restraints again, and I pull her back a little more forcefully.

"Believe me," I say to Megan, "we'll get something worthwhile out of you, but your summer homes won't cut it."

"What will?" says Delaney, innocence in her voice. I pull her closer into me, letting her practically rest against my chest, and I bring my face to her ear to speak to her.

"You'll see that soon enough, *chemo kargo*," I say, and she tightens her lips.

After what feels like hours, the van starts to pull up the dirt path leading to our little retreat. It's far from the public eye, concealed by mountains and woods that might have made our compound a perfect vacation spot. I glance up and out the front of the van, and I see our base of operations coming into view around the corner as the van rattles under us.

Once, this place was a Roman villa, an estate handed down from generations of landowners and eventually restored into a proper manor, complete with walls, vineyards, and gardens out front. I can practically picture the ritzy parties held here so long ago as I look upon the dilapidated, crumbling walls, the unruly beds of weeds that had once been gardens, and the remains of a cobblestone road leading into the place. The moonlight gave the place a haunting beauty. More importantly, the place was easily defensible, sitting on a hill that provided a stunning view of the Mediterranean, its high terraces and what remained of the walls making the place ideal for our operation.

We come to a stop at last, and while Megan's guard orders her to her feet, I simply pick up Delaney, and she gives a yelp as I carry her out of the van and hold her on her back in my arms, letting her legs dangle off to the side as she wiggles in her restraints.

As the other van is unloaded, my sharp ears catch a bit of what Caitlin is saying to her guard as he guides her out of the van. "...I mean it, I'd make it worth your while, big guy." There's a telltale lilt to her voice that I know well in women. So Caitlin is the fiery one of this group. I don't see in her the same guile I sense in Delaney, but she could be trouble.

I smile down at my captive, giving her a light squeeze while I carry her towards the estate's entrance, keeping out of earshot of the other girls. "Do you hear that? Your friend wants to play nice with my men. I'd warn her to be careful, if I were you," I say, lowering my tone as I lift her a little closer to me, and I can see her jaw clenching. "I'm the leader of this unsavory band of mine. But if your friend tries to play with fire, she might find herself in over her head. Of course," I add with a smile, "from the way you were talking to me earlier, I think you might like to play those dangerous games too, don't you?"

"Is that what this is about?" she says, and I'm amused to hear a sultry tone in her own voice this time. She's adaptable, this one. "There are easier ways to have a good time, you know. We can still help with that." She speaks boldly, but there's color to her cheeks that tells me delightful things about the hidden desires of the girl in my arms.

"As much as you'd like that, *sykhaara*," I tease, not giving her so much as an inch just yet, "that's not the case." My men leading the blindfolded girls behind me, I carry Delaney into the manor, where one of my men I'd left behind opens the door for us and nods, smiling at our catch. He knows better than to speak, though. Better if our girls don't know exactly how many of us there are.

I carry her up a flight of stairs, glancing at the wide, open entryway to the villa. The interior is even more worn-down than the outside. From the inside, you'd never know you were standing in what was once a lavish estate. We take the girls to the wing that was once a guest hall, lined with modest rooms with the windows that overlook a cliffside, should any of them get any poorly-planned ideas about escaping.

As the other men lead their women into their rooms, I carry Delaney into hers, closing the door behind me before setting her down on her feet, letting her steady herself before I remove her blindfold. She blinks, batting her long eyelashes as her eyes adjust to the lamplight. I smile at her as she regards me carefully, her mouth twisted in a frown as she starts to look around the place.

"These are your quarters," I explain, gesturing around. I follow her eyes to the cracked walls, their frescoes long-since faded, the high ceiling, the window, and the uncomfortable bed. Then she looks up at me, tugging at her wrist-bindings.

"Untie me, please," she asks, a slight whine in her voice, and I chuckle, ignoring her request.

"You will stay here, and your door will be locked until we take you out," I state, speaking slowly so she can catch every word. "If you behave yourself, little girl, then we might be kind and let you walk around the place of your own free will." I step forward, looming over her, and I take pleasure in the shiver I see run through her as I set my hands on her shoulders. "But you aren't used to behaving, are you? Look at you," I say, glancing up and down her expensive outfit, the makeup that must have come from Paris itself. "Does your daddy make you pout to get what you want, or does he like to pamper his little princess?"

She looks at me with shimmering eyes, a little color in her cheeks. Getting these rich girls hot is too easy. And with one so pretty as this, I find myself enjoying it more than usual.

"Why does that matter to you?" she whispers.

"It'll tell me how quickly he'll pay your ransom, of course," I say, and Delaney's eyes widen in understanding.

"You're...you're holding us hostage?" she breathes, and I can practically hear her heart beating faster.

"I knew you were the smart one," I tease, holding her chin with a thumb and forefinger pressing gently into those flushed cheeks, ever so gently. "Do you ever think about what that pretty body of yours is worth?" I say more than ask, letting a thumb brush over her lower lip. "If you're as much of a brat to your daddy as you are with me, then you'd better hope he's a forgiving man. Because I am not."

She swallows, her eyes full of fear as she tries to

make herself unreadable. It's almost pathetic. "They'll pay," she says, "I know they will. But if you do so much as lay a hand on us…"

I laugh at that, taking her by the arm and guiding her to her bed and sitting her down, putting a knee on the mattress and looming over her sitting form, her chest rising and falling even more quickly than before.

"What will happen? Do you think they'll pay less? Will their precious princess be too sullied for them?" I lean into her, looking her in the eye as she leans back slowly. "That wouldn't surprise me. You rich Americans are all the same. Think you've got the whole world wrapped around your pretty little finger," I say, slipping my hand around to hers and untying them, then taking one of her hands in mine and lifting it between us, enveloping her smaller one in mine. "Because everything has a price tag to you, doesn't it? Well, *sykhaara*, you have a price tag on yourself, now."

I pause to watch her reply, but she just stares up at me. Her thighs shift a little, trying to scoot back, but there's more than that in the motion. I can easily see what effect I'm having on her, and I can't say I'm not surprised. Girls might offer their body, but it's out of fear and desperation. While Delaney obviously feels both those things, I can sense her genuine interest as well.

"They'll pay," she finally repeats, quietly. "They're my parents. They love me."

"We will see," I muse, standing back up and stepping off the mattress, still glowering down at her. "But you know, you're a pretty thing — and we haven't sent out our demands just yet." I reach out and take a lock of her golden hair in my fingers, twirling it around again, a wicked smile on my face. "Maybe I'll keep you around as insurance to make sure the other girls are well behaved. Tell me, do you trust your friends enough for your life to be in their hands?"

"Do you trust your men enough not to fall for us?" she replies, and I feel a grin on my face despite myself.

"Oh, you're a special kind of spoiled brat, aren't you? No wonder the girls look up to you. Let me make something clear to you, then," I say, my voice growing deadly serious. "You're not in America anymore, Delaney. You're in our world now." I let my hard expression soften into a smirk. "But you're an interesting one. Maybe I'll keep you for myself, forget about the whole ransom altogether. You might just prove to be more valuable than your price tag. But we'll have to do something about that attitude of yours, first," I tease, letting her hair fall from my fingers as she does her best to keep it together. "A few hours ago, the idea of being mine seemed exciting to you. How about now?"

I can tell that I've pushed her to the brink — exactly where I want her, though it tempts me sorely to push her just a little further.

I step back, keeping my eyes on her as she pulls her legs up on the bed, wrapping her arms around herself as her gorgeous blue eyes watch me, a mix of emotions laced with terror in that expression.

"Behave yourself, little girl," I say, opening the door behind me, shooting her a wink as I start to step out into the hall. "If you don't, I might have to come tie you down to that bed myself."

This has to be a nightmare.

As I lie in the uncomfortable bed in the corner of my aged holding cell, I stare up at the cracked ceiling and will myself to wake up. This cannot be happening. None of this can possibly be real. What has happened to me in the past thirty-six hours is the kind of thing I see in thrilling documentaries. Girls being captured by greedy, lascivious men and ransomed out for their parents' cash. Girls being deceived, blinded by handsome faces, led directly into the waiting jaws of the shark. I can't help but feel like we all walked the plank, somehow, like we've all made this choice ourselves.

And we only have ourselves to blame, don't we?

I screw my eyes shut tightly, frantically trying to block out my surroundings. Maybe I was just in a coma or something and I would wake up any moment now and everything would be fine. I would be back at home in my luxurious four-poster bed.

But when I open my eyes, my heart sinks. I'm still in this ancient ruin of a bedroom, surrounded by faded walls and that dank, musty smell. This place was probably once something terribly beautiful. Something worth preserving. But now it only holds distant echoes of its former beauty and vitality. Oh, and it holds *me*.

I turn over in bed, fighting the sting of tears threatening to pool up in my eyes. I can't give into that just yet. I'm tougher than this. I'm no average whiny spoiled rich girl from the States. Oh, no. These guys may think they've broken my spirit and crushed me down into some docile little mouse, and it may be better to let them think that for now, but I know I'm more than that. I've always been more than people bargain for when they first look at me. I'm deeper and stronger than the pretty, innocent face I wear lets on. And I'll be damned if I let a pack of filthy horndog criminals cow me into silence and obedience.

Still, it can't hurt to let them believe they have won. I learned a long, long time ago that when people underestimate me, I should take it as a gift. I give people exactly what they expect, which lures them into a false sense of security, believing they've got me all figured out. It leaves them vulnerable to any surprises I have in store.

It's a technique I remember from a book I read as a kid — back when I was a giant nerd — Sun Tzu's *The Art of War*. I distinctly recall the lines: Do what people expect; it's what they're able to see easiest and confirms their biases. It settles them into predictable responses, busying their minds while you wait for the right moment — the one they aren't expecting.

It's been my mantra for years, as I grew into a newer, stronger person. A version of myself which reflects back exactly what people expect of me, playing so expertly into their stereotypes, that people have forgotten who I used to be. No one remembers the twelve-year-old Delaney who wore thick glasses and was painfully rejected by her first love in front of everyone. Now, I am powerful. I am self-assured. But I can play the damsel or the debutante with ease. I'm an actress, playing which-ever role will benefit me most in any given situa-tion. I can be whoever I need to be, at the drop of a hat.

I ponder over Sun Tzu's words as I curl up in bed, forcing myself not to dwell on the fact that I am outnumbered and overpowered here. I know there are at least ten men involved in this operation, and I'm not foolish enough to think there aren't at least several more skulking around this old building quietly. I'm sure Darios wants me to feel like I have a chance. He wants to do the same thing to me that

I'm doing to him: he wants to make me underestimate him, even just a little bit.

But I know by now how exactly to size up my enemies. Of course, throughout my experiences the majority of my "enemies" have been quite a bit more harmless. Mostly other girls who hoped to overthrow the Popular Girl Empire I've established for myself, and none of that can really help me now, can it?

I'm not in Savannah anymore. I don't have my legions of envious girls and lustful boys to help me here. All I have are my three closest friends, and my wits. And my friends are kept separately from me. In fact, I can't even know for sure that they're still in the building. This horrifying thought jolts me back to the present moment and I suddenly feel sick to my stomach. This is my fault. I'm the one who suggested the four of us have a wild weekend in Spain without anyone's knowledge or permission. I'm the one who paid for the room and the cab. I'm the one who led us directly into this death trap.

I swallow hard, trying not to think about how much trouble I've caused.

But god, if anything were to happen to any of my friends… it would be all my fault.

"No," I murmur aloud to myself. "I won't let them hurt my friends any more than they already have. If I'm the one who got us into this mess, then I damn well ought to be the one who gets us back out again."

Just then, there's a knock at my door and I gasp aloud, sitting up straight in bed with my heart hammering away in my chest. The door creaks open and I start instinctively backing away, sliding off the bed to stumble away into the back corner of the room. As if that small distance could possibly save me, anyway.

A tall, dark male figure steps into the room and I immediately recognize his hulking frame: it's Darios. He gives me a cool smile, a flash of satisfaction in his eyes when he sees me cowering in the corner. I inwardly slap myself for being so predictable. I've given him exactly what he wants — to see me break down and fear him.

But that just means it's time to play that card.

"*Dila mshvidobisa*, Delaney," he greets, with a faux-gentlemanly tilt of his head. I damn myself for still thinking him so attractive, even though I now know the true nature of the darkness behind his eyes. I can't let him see that, though. It would be unexpected, and something he'd use against me.

"What do you want?" I whimper, holding my own head up high. But I let him see me just a little vulnerable, my hands fidgeting at my sides. He hones in on that small gesture immediately, and I know he's already thinking he's won. He's beaten me. But two can play this game of chicken.

"Oh, come now. Can't a man check in on his best girl without some ulterior motive?" Darios asks, spreading his arms open in a gesture of apology. I fold my arms over my chest and poke out my bottom lip ever so slightly, giving him a defiant, petulant-little-girl look.

"I am not your girl," I shoot back, glaring daggers at him.

I can tell he's at least a little surprised by my response, but instead of being bothered by it, he merely looks pleased. He takes several steps closer and beckons for me to come over to him, but I dig into my position more firmly.

"Now don't play coy with me, little girl. I have some lovely news," he announces, grinning brilliantly. But on him, the smile is less like a pleasantry and far more dangerous and threatening.

"What? Just come out with it," I spit, never letting my eyes break away from his.

"Oh, you're in a nasty mood today, I see. But relax. We are going on a little outing, you and me. Well, it's more like a double date, I suppose," he remarks, shrugging.

My thoughts immediately sprint off in a thousand different directions. He's not doing very much to make this prospect sound harmless, and I can tell it's actually some kind of veiled threat. Perhaps a double date is merely a way of saying he and one of his men doing something downright awful to me and one of my friends. I gulp back a knot of anxiety.

"Please don't hurt my friends," I plead softly, my

armor softening for a split second. Even though I liked to play it cool, I really, truly adored my friends. And I feel a heavy burden of responsibility for them, especially now.

Darios chuckles grimly and reaches out with lightning-quick reflexes to grab hold of my arm and snatch me close. "Don't you worry. None of your poor little rich girls are going to be harmed too severely on my watch. In fact, I've got a wonderful surprise in store for your friend Megan today."

My stomach twists and turns. Not sweet, dim Megan. Of course he would single out the weakest link first. "And what might that be?" I ask, almost too afraid to listen to the answer.

"She's going home," Darios replies simply.

"Wh-what?" I stammer, so surprised that I forget my ice queen demeanor for a moment.

He pulls me away out the door, his fingers forming an iron grip on my arm as we go. He drags me down the hallway and down a set of rickety stairs. In the lobby at the bottom of the stairs are two burly men from last night, each of them holding Megan by her arms. She looks up at the sound of our footsteps and an expression of wide-eyed familiarity jumps onto her face.

"Delaney! You're okay!" she bursts out, straining to get closer to me. But the two men hold her perfectly still. "I was so worried they hurt you or something. Oh god, I'm so scared."

"Shh, it's alright. You're gonna be just fine," I console her. Darios laughs.

"That's an understatement. Congratulations, Megan, you get to be the first to go home to your parents," he declares.

"What?" my friend gasps, looking back and forth between us in shock. "Delaney, did you convince him to do this? I knew you would come through! And you're coming with us, so that must mean you're going home, too!"

"Oh, no such luck for Miss Delaney," Darios interrupts, shaking his head. "She's just tagging along as, ah, let's just call her 'insurance.'"

"So you best behave," growls one of the other men in Megan's ear. She shudders visibly.

The men pile us all into one van and we start driving toward civilization. The crumbling villa disappears behind us as we drive down the hill. Megan is seated next to me in the back and she scoots closer to rest her head on my shoulder, her hand slipping into mine. I can feel her trembling fearfully. One of the men sits across from us, his expression stony-faced.

The whole ride there, the two men in the front speak softly and rapidly in a foreign language that sounds vaguely Russian or possibly even Greek. Either way, it is totally beyond me, and so instead I focus on comforting Megan. Finally, after what feels like an eternity of driving, we pass into the city, the looming buildings of Barcelona on either side. The van pulls to a stop outside a little cafe, and while Darios stays in the driver's seat, the other two men jump out and come around to escort Megan out and into the restaurant.

She turns to look at me, mouthing the word *help* as they latch onto her arms and pull her away, leaving me alone in the van with Darios. I instinctively start to get up to go after her, but my dark stranger clucks his tongue and shakes his head at me.

"Don't even think about it, *bavshvi*," he leers warningly.

"Are they going to hurt her?" I ask, clenching my fists at my sides, unable to fully conceal my genuine concern for my sweetest friend. Darios rolls his beautiful brown eyes.

"Of course not. I doubt her parents would like to buy back damaged goods now, would they? From what my research tells me, they are shrewd business-people. They know the value of an item," he comments, and I feel rage burning in my gut at the fact that he is regarding the four of us like we're nothing but merchandise. But I have to remain calm. I can't let him see how much he bothers me. We're both fumbling for the upper hand here.

"When do we get to go in?" I press him.

"Patience, little girl. First we wait for Mr. and Mrs. Reece to show up, and then you and I will make our move. But here is the thing, Delaney. You and I must act like we are merely two people on a date. If you so much as forget to smile, I will make sure you and your friend regret it," he warns darkly.

At just that moment, I see through the tinted window of the van that Megan's parents are nervously shuffling into the restaurant. "They're here, that's them," I remark.

"I know. But we must not move too quickly, lest they catch onto us. You and I will follow them in and sit down at the corner table. You will order tea and a salad, and you *will* smile," Darios commands, slowly getting out of the front seat and coming round to help me out. From the second my feet hit the pavement, Darios's entire demeanor shifts. Suddenly, his dark clouds are lifted and he gives me an electrifying grin, squeezing my hand fondly as he raises it to his lips.

It's unnerving. He's nearly as good of an actor as me, and I have to wonder how long he's been practicing. I have 5 years of solid study under my belt, though, and I'm not going to let him win this little game.

He gently kisses the top of my hand before leading me into the restaurant and I flutter my lashes at him. Just as he instructed, we take our seats at the corner table. Out of the corner of my eye I can see Megan and her parents seated at a booth across the restaurant, her parents huddled in the seat across from them looking absolutely terrified. There is a big brown suitcase propped on the table and the men are talking in low voices. I wish I could read their lips from here, but before I even get a chance to try, Darios is squeezing my hand again.

He hisses, "Look at me. Not at them. Remember, we must be thoroughly convincing. One wrong move and I will tear this entire operation apart."

A pretty waitress steps up to our table and introduces herself in Spanish, asking what we would like to eat. Darios orders a sandwich and a beer and then gently pressed his thumb into the palm of my hand, urging me to order. I glance down at the menu, which is conveniently open to the page depicting various types of salad.

"Oh — um, could I have — I mean, *la ensalada con fresas y un té, por favor*," I say with a tender smile. The waitress nods sweetly and hurries away to put in our order.

"Good choice," Darios remarks, giving me a fond smile which does not match the coldness in his dark eyes. "The strawberry salad is fantastic."

"What is going to happen to Megan now?" I whisper.

Anger flashes in Darios's eyes. "Don't worry about that. You're not here to keep an eye on her. I am. Just sit there and look pretty."

Our food arrives soon and we both eat, even though I'm feeling downright nauseous. I've never been a fan of hot tea, much preferring the sweet tea I grew up with in Savannah, but when Darios eyes the untouched cup menacingly, I quickly take a sip.

I know it's easier for him to appear calm in this situation, even content. He has the upper hand and he knows it. But there's a chance coming up for me, and I smile sweetly and eat my salad as I bide my time.

Throughout our meal, Darios is shockingly kind and attentive to the waitress, even making harmless small talk with her in fluent Spanish. It's not flirtatious either, I'm an expert on that, and there's not a lick of it to be noticed. I'm not quite able to keep up, as I am nowhere near fluent, plus I'm a little distracted by the actual ransom trade-off going down across the room.

"Pay attention to me, not them," Darios orders, through a smile. "You can't see it right now, and neither can anyone else because of this lovely checkered tablecloth, but I'm pointing a gun at you under the table."

My blood runs cold as I realize that he's not lying. One of his hands has been under the table, out of sight, for the entirety of our time here. I can't believe I didn't even pick up on it until now. I've let my guard down, and now I'm paying the price. So I give him a falsely adoring smile and tilt my head to one side slightly, giggling as though he's said something very funny.

I realize once more that I'm out of my league. I thought that I could scream and let the entire restaurant know I'm being held hostage once Megan and her family have left, but he snatched that chance away from me. I can't do anything but wait and pray.

Out of the corner of my eye, I can see movement happening at the table where Megan is seated with her guards. Before I can stop myself, I look over and in a flash instant, I notice something that sends a little thrill of hope through my body.

There's something black poking out of one of the guards' shirts. And I've watched enough true crime television shows to know what it is.

A wire. One of the guys is wearing a wire; a listening device. And something tells me Darios's operation is not the type to engage in that kind of subterfuge — he seems like a more old-fashioned criminal. But as soon as I turn back to look at Darios, I see that he, too, has noticed the wire. And there is an expression of dark, brooding rage in his eyes. Is there a traitor in his midst?

We Georgians look out for each other here in Spain. We have expanded so very far from our homeland because our network's influence has extended through sheer willpower and guile. Branches like the one I run are so remote that they are virtually independent, and the sole uniting factor that keeps us together, despite our occasional power struggles, is our devotion to one another based on our ethnicity.

So when there is a traitor among us, the punishment must be dealt swiftly and harshly.

It broke my heart to see Sandro wearing a wire in that restaurant. Even so, on the ride back to the compound, it had been a struggle not to take out my pistol and blow him away before we even got out of the city. But that isn't how I handle my business.

Once the van pulls up to the compound, I look to

Delaney, whose uneasy gaze is watching me carefully. She's seen the wire too, and she understood what it meant. She's smart and perceptive, and that makes things more difficult for me.

I crack a smile at her. Bringing her along with me as I did might have made her more jittery than I'd have liked, but it was necessary. The more I could bring her out in the city and show her I could still keep an eye on her, the less likely she was to run and endanger my whole operation.

Besides, the little princess was probably suffering without a daily expensive meal out on the town. And I enjoy playing with this one.

Sandro starts to unload Delaney with the other men to take her to her room, but I speak up before he can slip away, where he would undoubtedly bring his evidence to the attention of the authorities. "Ambrosi, you take the little lady to her quarters. Davit, Sandro, you two come with me. I want the money secured before we turn in for the night."

The two men exchange glances and nod, and Delaney watches me as she's taken away. The look in her eyes is something that piques my interest. I know she saw me notice Sandro's wire. It would be the easiest thing in the world for her to warn him right now, tip him off in some way. Either way, it would only result in his death, but it might give her some struggling attempt at grasping for power while under my control. Yet as Ambrosi leads her away, she doesn't take her chance. She eventually lets her gaze be turned away to the front door of the estate as I watch her go.

The men clamber back into the van, Davit clutching the briefcase of money as we get in and pull back out again.

From here on out, keeping Sandro calm is the priority. The slightest hint that I know about him could spook him and make this situation infinitely more dangerous. He's armed, after all. Davit's presence is purely to ease his nerves, since it's normal for us to make drop-offs in threes as to minimize the risk of betrayal. Only a handful of my men are entrusted with the location of our dead drop. After today, that number will be one less.

"Good call, suggesting we take a bunch of girls from the same traveling group," Davit says to Sandro as we start down the road. I'm sitting in the passenger's seat while he drives, Davit in the back. Credit where credit was due — this had been his idea from the start. "Boss, did you see the panic in those parents' eyes? How much you want to bet all the parents are feeding off each other's panic over the whole situation?"

"I was a little distracted with my hostage," I say in a bemused tone, scratching my jaw with a smile. "But they looked spooked from what I did see. Well done."

"Thanks, Boss," Sando says, but through his tone, I can hear anxiety. This game is far from over.

"You getting distracted more and more with her around, Boss?" Davit asks, chuckling in the back, but I shoot him a glare over my shoulder that shuts him up.

"Are you kidding? Spoiled brat like her? The only distraction is how stubborn the girl is," I lie, my mind drifting to the feel of her sides in my hands. If it weren't for the gun under the table, that might have been a very nice date out on the town. But then again, making a rich girl like her squirm was almost as entertaining in and of itself.

"I could stand to distract myself with that for a little while," Davit chuckles, and I feel an angry boiling in my blood, and I give a sharp grunt.

"You touch the merchandise, you'll lose those quick fingers with talk like that," I say, and Davit quickly shuts up. This is a helpful distraction from what's on Sandro's mind, but I feel the strange desire to sincerely get them to back off from Delaney. If someone's going to toy with her, it will be me. Smiling, I add in a lighter tone, "Just think of the payoff and save your energy for buying a few nights of fun up in France when we're done with all this."

"You know, for all the times we've transported cargo through the country, I've never stopped in France," Sandro muses, glancing out the window at the Spanish countryside whizzing by. We've driven far enough that we're starting to see vineyards in the hills off to the side of the road, rolling hills dotted with people tending the grapes. We have a little ways yet to go, into a more remote part of the mountains.

"Nor have I," I say, following his gaze. "Never had the chance."

"Didn't have parents who liked to travel?" Sandro asks, raising an eyebrow with a smile. It's a half-joke, I know, and I smile back. I'm not subtle about my distaste for tourists. It's part of what's made me so 'energetic' about my newfound passion here in Spain.

"You've been to the capital back home, Sandro? Tbilisi?"

"Of course."

"On the outskirts of the city on the north side, there's a slum that used to be both a home for the factory workers and a refuge for political refugees. Easy place to disappear, if you didn't mind the rats and didn't get too close to the open sewer lines. That's where I grew up. My friends and I, we played on the rusted assembly lines of abandoned factories that no longer had a purpose after the fall of the Soviet Union." I chuckle, thinking back to what seemed like a brighter time. "We'd have fights in the alleys behind what I think used to be a rug factory. They had a big fenced-in parking lot back there, so we could make ourselves a little arena."

"Bunch of little thugs, you were," Davit laughs.

"Oh, you're one to talk — didn't your parents raise you in a carnival?" Sandro chuckles back.

"Only for a few years," Davit says modestly.

"We drove out the thugs, actually," I say, putting my hands behind my head and smiling. "Our pack of boys hit our teen years and grew so vicious that even the petty criminals didn't dare come around our turf. Wasn't long before the mafia started scouting us out."

"Any of them get left behind?" Sandro asks, raising an eyebrow.

"No," I say, a wistful tone behind the word. "Richer, younger families started to move in not long after I left — it started just after I was sent to prison, but before the war. Now, none of the poor families can afford the place anymore."

The other men grunt their distaste. I know they've felt the sting of similar experiences. The rich do all they can to crowd the poor majority out of the world.

Eventually, after a few more minutes of reminiscing, we come to a stop on a dirt road in a forest and start taking sixty paces off the road to the east, coming to a small hole in the ground we've covered with brush. Sandro takes the spade I hand him, and he starts digging.

After a few minutes, as Davit and I stride around the area to make sure we're not being watched, I hear the sound of Sandro's spade hitting metal, and I stride over towards him. He brushes the rest of the dirt off a metal door we had put in, and he pulls out the key to the padlock on it to unlock our dead drop.

The padlock clicks open at the same time as I cock my gun, and with a dull 'thud' of my silenced pistol, Sandro's lifeless body hits the ground unceremoniously, his blood on the tree in front of him, face buried in the dead drop hole.

Davit rushes over, eyes wide and looking around as he takes his gun out, looking for the attacker, but when he sees my raised pistol and the grave nod I give him, he understands, and his face goes ashen.

He knows not to question me, but I gesture to Sandro's body. "Open his shirt." Davit steps forward and obeys, and as he unbuttons Sandro's shirt, his face blanches even more at the sight of the wire on his chest.

"Dampalo dzaghlo," he curses through gritted teeth, standing up and punching a nearby tree, making his knuckles bleed. Davit has always been a hot-blooded one, like me.

I step forward, patting him on the shoulder briefly before ripping the wire off Sandro's body and checking the recorder. "Cheap Spaniards couldn't even spare the expense for a live feed — this is on an old tape recording.

I pull out a lighter and hold the flame to the device, letting it melt and warp, the film bursting into flame, destroying any and all evidence that

Sandro planned to bring to whomever put him up to this.

"Can't be INTERPOL, they would have a better budget than this," Davit says after he regains his bearings. I nod in agreement.

"Bury the body here," I say, gesturing a few feet away from the dead drop. "I'll instruct our comrades to pick him up tomorrow night with the payload." Davit nods as I feel my phone buzzing, and as he drags his friend's body away, I put the phone to my ear.

"Yes?"

"Boss, we have a problem," comes Ambrosi's flustered voice over the phone.

"Just took care of one, I'd like to see you top it," I say, glancing over to Davit.

"It's the head girl — Delaney," he says, and I feel my heart jump to my throat. "I left her in her room to get her lunch, and when I came back, she was gone — there's a rope made of bedsheets leading out the window. She's climbed down the cliffs."

Fuck, I curse silently as my jaw clenches. "Stay calm. I'm on my way."

* * *

IT WAS a miracle we weren't pulled over as I tore down the road, Davit clutching his seat nervously at my driving, but I'm not about to let this one slip through my fingers. It was a long drive out here, and by the time we're approaching the villa, it's nearly sunset.

"Think she'll make it far?" Davit asks.

"Are you kidding?" I snort, despite my driving. "The pampered little girl couldn't find her way in the city without help. I'm more worried she'll die out in the wilderness, then there goes our pay for the month."

"No doubt," Davit agrees with a chuckle, "knowing the Americans, she'll wander back to the villa after a few minutes of starting to sunburn."

I smile, but there's a greater worry in me. If she made it out of the compound, she's put some thought into this — guard patrols have to be memorized, certain work has to be done quietly, when nobody is listening, she would have had to climb down the villa wall at a time when nobody would be walking about outside…I'm starting to suspect this Delaney girl is sharper than she let on. My smile becomes a little more genuine.

It's been awhile since I've had a worthy game of cat and mouse to deal with. But I wonder how she will fare out in the cliffs? Maybe I ought to give her something of a head start before I go after her.

We pull up at the compound, and Davit gets out with me as Ambrosi steps up to greet us, his face flushed.

"I'll deal with your punishment later," I tell

Ambrosi in a firm voice before he has time to ask where Sandro is. I figure it will make my point a little sharper. He starts to speak, but simply nods after a moment.

"Shall I organize a hunting party, sir?" Davit says, looking up at the setting sun. "I can have a score of men out here in an hour or so if you-"

"No," I cut him off, slipping out of my jacket, handing it to Ambrosi, and rolling my sleeves up my thick forearms. "I will handle this myself. Tend to the other girls. Make sure word of this doesn't get around."

Davit blinks in disbelief, but then he nods, gesturing for Ambrosi to follow him. "Yes, Boss."

Walking at a brisk pace, I head for the exit of the estate, around to the cliffs. It's time for a little hike.

I've never run so fast in my entire life, not even during cheerleading practice back when I was still focused on being the squad captain. I almost want to laugh for thinking the stakes had been high for me then, in comparison to what I'm dealing with now.

The full moon is rising overhead, a luminous orb gazing down at me ominously through the veil of dark tree branches high above me. Judging me for my terrible choices. Watching me fall apart. My breaths are coming raggedly now, the ache of fatigue in my legs reaching an unbearable pitch. I feel my lungs tightening up as I run out of stamina, every nerve in my body telling me to slow down, to stop.

I don't know how long I've been running or how far I've gotten. I'm not even sure which direction I've been going this whole time. If only I had stayed in

Girl Scouts as a child, maybe I would know how to follow the stars or the moon or something helpful. Maybe I wouldn't be so terrified right now. Of course, I don't think even the Girl Scouts could have prepared me for being kidnapped and held for ransom by a wickedly handsome criminal in a foreign country. And I'm realizing now, to my surprise, that the woods outside Barcelona don't look anything like the homey forests of my native Georgia.

Even the trees here loom menacingly around me, the cool earth underfoot tripping me left and right as I run. And I won't be able to go on much longer at this pace. That is for certain.

Finally, my knees start to buckle underneath me and I give into the signals my body is desperately sending me, coming to a rough halt and collapsing clumsily in a pile of leaves. The air is shockingly cool considering the fact that it's summertime, and despite how warm my body is from such extreme exertion, I can feel chill bumps rising up along my arms.

"Where the hell am I?" I mumble aloud, looking around in confused horror. I am starting to regret my spontaneous decision to just bust out of the villa and go gallivanting off into the night with no real idea of where I'm going. I can't believe my own stupidity, thinking I could just pull a cinematic move like this. Knotting my bedsheets into a makeshift rope? Climbing down the outer wall of the villa like some action-film version of Rapunzel?

I'm definitely going to die out here, aren't I?

I don't know if I've been running toward or away from civilization, but it certainly feels like the city of Barcelona is nowhere near here. All I can see is endless forest in every direction, like I've just been plucked up and unceremoniously dropped into the wilderness. I pull my knees in close to my chest, trying to calm the galloping beat of my heart. I'm stronger than this. I can't let fear rule me this way. I'll never survive unless I get a grip.

But with the night settling in like a thick black shroud around me, it's hard to keep my thoughts from wandering down dark, calamitous paths. I can't help but think back to that murderous glint in Darios's eyes when he noticed the wire one of his men was wearing. I shudder to myself, wondering what kind of punishment the guy endured.

I have no doubt in my mind that Darios would kill someone who crossed him.

And that realization is enough to spur me back to my feet and keep going. If he was that intensely angry at one of his own cohorts, then there was no telling how furious he would be with someone like me for defying him. I could only imagine the hatred in his dark eyes as he wrapped his hands around my throat. Or would he simply shoot me? After all, he did spend our entire fake lunch date pointing a gun at me under the tablecloth. For all I know, he could be out here looking for me right now.

I have to keep moving if I want to live.

I trudge through the woods, my initial adrenaline rush tapering away as the agony in my bare feet starts to prickle at the edges of my consciousness. I almost wish I had brought my shoes with me, but I know I would not have gotten very far in heels. At the moment, going barefoot definitely feels like a mistake, as well. I glance down hesitantly and wince at the sight of my cut-up, bruised, filthy feet. Back home in Georgia I never would have dreamed of going without shoes. It's disgusting. But it's funny how quickly your perspective changes once you're dropped into immediate danger.

If only I had my phone with me right now, I think to myself, I could try and dial someone's number — anyone. But it dawns on me that my parents are undoubtedly in Europe by now, and they always buy disposable international devices instead of bringing their usual iPhones when they go on big trips like this one. So I wouldn't know their new phone numbers anyway. I rack my brain, trying to think of who I would call if I had the chance. Besides, who could tell what lay beyond the edges of this deep, dark forest? Perhaps there was a public phone I could use. I could run into some business and beg to use their phone. But who would I call?

It hits me that the only people I ever call are my

three closest friends, all of whom are currently in similar states of peril. Megan is presumably safe and sound with her parents now, but I'm sure the guards never gave her back her phone. And on top of that, I highly doubt her parents would ever let her get in contact with any of us again. I'm sure Darios's men warned them not to try anything. I couldn't tell what was being said at that table in the restaurant, but I know some threats were probably made, and the Reeces would know better than to try and make contact with any of us girls now. I feel a pang of pity for Megan, even though she's the only one of us I know for sure is safe, because I know she must be feeling terrible knowing she can't help us. She may be a bit dim-witted, but she's very compassionate toward her friends.

And if I can't call my friends and I can't call my parents... well, that really only leaves one person: my now ex-boyfriend Brandon. My stomach churns at the thought of having to go crawling back to him for help. Even in this dark, morbid state I still loathe the idea of reaching out to him. He was the one who tried to convince me not to go to Europe this summer, with or without my parents. Brandon cited many reasons, each of them more insulting than the last.

"It's too dangerous out there for someone like you," he'd said, fixing me with that familiar condescending gaze. He continued, "What if you get separated from your parents? What if you get lost? Laney, sweetheart, you wouldn't last five minutes alone in a foreign country. Besides, you would miss me too much. We're supposed to be together forever, you know? And what kind of future wife of mine would simply run off to another country all summer? If you leave me here, I'll be lonely and you know you will be, too. And when *I* get lonely I start looking around for someone else to make me feel better, if you know what I mean. It's not my fault, it's just the way guys are, honey."

Needless to say, I had broken up with him almost immediately. After approximately four years of dating. The look on his face when I told him it was over almost made up for the fact that he had just insulted my competence and threatened to cheat on me in one fell swoop. I don't think he ever expected me to dump him. Brandon truly believed the lie, the persona I'd created; that I was a waifish damsel just waiting to be bossed around and manipulated by some buttoned-up prince charming for the rest of my happily ever after. Hell, everyone else assumed the two of us would get married straight out of high school, too. We were prom king and queen. We were Danny and Sandy. We were everybody's favorite high school sweethearts.

And I threw it all away in an instant.

I don't regret it, even now. My crush on Brandon at thirteen had dissipated around age fifteen when I realized he was just a regular, generic douchebag with an exceptionally handsome face. Boys like him were a dime a dozen, but it suited my purposes to keep him around for a while. Not only did I get to coast by on his own popularity status, but I gained access to the entire football team, which in turn gave me the chance to infiltrate the cheerleading squad and become the captain. And once I reached that position, there was no turning back.

I was in. No, more than that; I was *it*.

Of course, none of that makes much of a difference now that I'm darting barefoot through the wilds of Catalonia with a probable serial murderer hot on my trail. My alpha hot girl status can't make me run any faster or figure out which direction I'm supposed to go.

As I bolt through the trees, trying to ignore the sharp needles of pain in my feet, I realize that now the thing I have hidden from the world for years is the one thing that might actually help me survive out here: my wits. I have spent the last six years of my life burying my mind, playing dumb, acting the innocent, and now I have to remember who I used to be. It's time to shed my fake identity and be real, for once. It's the only hope I have for getting out of this alive.

DARIOS

I breathe deeply, looking out over the rocks that descend into more forest toward the coast. My eyes scan the tops of the trees, looking for signs of movement down in the shadowy forest. I wonder how much fear must be racking the poor girl's mind, out here alone in the forest with naught but the howling of wolves to keep her company.

I don't plan to lose my catch out here. Not tonight, not to the wilderness. There's something nagging at the back of my mind, though, something more than the simple urge to take back a young lady who's worth her weight in gold. I find myself thinking about her safety out here. She's a small woman, and she would be out of her element on the best of days in the woods of her own homeland. From her immaculately styled hair to her polished nails, she's a pampered girl who's never had to worry about such things, but there's some cunning in her I haven't seen in the others. And she was not content to stick around like a sheep at the villa.

I can't ignore the fact that Delaney *planned* this escape, short-sighted though it was. She didn't just run at the first chance she got, there was some real thought that went into this escape attempt. And if I can't find her soon, she might just succeed.

I snort as I stride across the cliff, keeping my eyes alert. Why do I feel protective over such a brat? Nevertheless, I have no plans of letting her outwit me tonight.

After what feels like hours, my eyes catch a flash of blonde darting through the trees, her hair betraying her in the full moon's light. I smile. I can see the way she's going — whether she knows it or not, she's running through an old hunter's trail. Deer had been chased down that trail for centuries if not millennia by huntsmen. I was amused at the thought of me as the huntsman, her my prey.

I move quickly, running up ahead of the path to cut her off. Every now and then, I spot her moving through the woods. She looks terrified, and she keeps looking over her shoulder at the faintest snap of a twig. With good reason. The dangers of the woods at night were not to be taken lightly by seasoned woodsmen, much less foolish little girls who can't find their way out of a crowded mall without guidance.

The cliff starts to get lower after I pass her, eventually leveling off to the same elevation as Delaney, and I can hear her footsteps and panicked breathing getting closer. Good that I'm finding her when I am — much longer out alone like this, and she'd descend into panic. It's already nearly pitch-black out here, save for the spots where the moonlight shines through the forest canopy. I get down low to the ground as I near the path, and I take cover by a fallen tree near where I suspect she's coming.

I hear her footsteps padding closer, and I can tell by the sound of her breath that she's nearly on me. Then there's a moment's hesitation, and I can practically taste in the air the same pause a deer feels the moment it can't see or hear its predator but suddenly, inexplicably realizes it's being hunted.

Delaney was already turning heel to run away when I rise up from behind the log, but my arms catch her easily as she lets out a scream, pounding her little fists against me and struggling against my arms as I pull her close to me.

"No, no!" she shouts, kicking at my shins with bare feet as I try to get a hold of her arms and pin them to her sides, chuckling at her efforts. "Damn you, no!"

As she struggles, I catch a glimpse of her eyes and realize there's mortal fear in them, and once I've hugged her to my front, squeezing her still for just a moment, I can feel her heart pounding fiercely against me, her breath seizing up. She's starting to have a panic attack.

"Shh, little princess, shh," I hush her, but she starts thrashing again, trying to get away. At last, I release her body, holding onto one of her arms with a grip that I know she can't hope to break away from. With a pained grunt, she struggles away, pulling and jerking her shoulder, and I frown, scooping her up again. "You're going to dislocate your shoulder," I chide her.

"What do you care?" she snaps, trying to kick at me with her legs while I hold her. "Just...just get this over with, will you?"

I raise an eyebrow at her, perplexed, but then I see her looking up at me defiantly. I've seen that look before. She expects that I came out her to kill her for her disobedience. The look in her face is that of someone ready to face death, and it's not a look that cowards have it in them to produce.

This girl gets more interesting by the hour.

I find myself laughing quietly despite myself, and Delaney's face goes bright red, and she reaches up to strike me again, but I catch her, setting her down on her feet and gently restraining her arms as she tries to hit me.

"Quit laughing, you sadist! What are you laughing about?"

"Poor girl," I say, "do you think I would have chased you down all the way out here to kill you? If I'd wanted you dead, well, you're already doing a good job of making that happen, running out into the forest at night with nothing but a dress. Don't you know," I add, a grin on my face as I lift her chin to face me, "there are wolves prowling about at night."

There are tears in her eyes, and I realize that I might have pushed her too far. She thrashes out against me again, but I can feel that her body is too tired to put up much of a fight.

"Why do you always do that?" she pouts, her voice choked by a sob.

"Do what?" I ask as she starts to calm down, her breathing getting slower and steadier.

"You trivialize everything that happens to us! To me!" she says, a couple of heavy tears rolling down her face. "I've been going through hell because of you, and you're laughing at me! I could have died tonight for all I knew, and you're just laughing it off like...like I'm some-"

"Petulant little American who's never known a day of hardship in her life before now?" I answer, narrowing my eyes. Her lip quivers, and still, she looks beautiful in the moonlight, her pouting face challenging me with its stare. I could kiss that frown away.

Despite myself, I do not feel my heart hardening

against her plight as I usually do. She's ignorant, that's something she can't deny...but it's also something she can't help. And in her, I see a hint of something more. Some kind of potential beyond the airheaded whims of an upper-class spoiled girl.

"Come with me," I say, releasing one of her arms and slipping my hand down to hold her smaller one, enveloping it entirely in a firm but gentle grip.

"Do I have a choice?" she mutters as I lead her along, minding her step a little more. I lead her a short walk south, being careful to take paths that are not riddled with sharp twigs and thorns. The poor girl came out here with bare legs that are already covered in little cuts. After a few minutes, Delaney is still too shaken up to question our destination. The treeline breaks, the smell of salty air reaches us, and there's a slope that leads down to the lapping waves that crash against the sandy shore of the Mediterranean.

The full moon casts a gorgeous road of moonlight over the waters, and with Delaney's hand in mine, I feel her heartbeat start to settle, perhaps calmed by the sounds of crashing waves. I give her an unreadable glance before leading her down the slope, towards the waves.

"You were a short walk from the shore. You might have followed it to safety, rather than die alone in the woods," I say once we're down there. A light breeze washes over us, and Delaney's first instinct is to move closer into me, but she catches herself and steps back, her cheeks reddening as I grin down at her.

"So are you just taking me down here to show me what I *could* have done right?" she says ruefully, frowning out at the waters. "Prove to me that I'm just a scared little girl without daddy?" she adds, imitating my accent, and I give her hand a warning squeeze that makes her drop her defiant expression.

"I already knew that," I tease, and she reaches out to slap my chest again, but I catch her other hand, leaving us standing like dancers in the middle of a waltz on the beach as the waves lap up over her feet in the sand as she looks up at me with pouting eyes.

"Where do you suppose I am from, Delaney?"

She furrows her brow, and I can see her trying to figure out if this is some kind of verbal trap. "I...I don't know. Greece? Russia?"

I tut, raising my eyebrows. "Careful, girl. I'm a forgiving man, but accuse my men of being Russians, and you might find yourself in hot water I can't save you from."

"You've been the one putting me in hot water all this time!"

"I saved you just now, didn't I?" I return, and she pauses. I smile. "It hurts, doesn't it? To be powerless no matter how hard you fight back? I know the feeling well, believe it or not, but people like you? You could go your whole life without it."

She stares at me as I nod down the coastline toward the direction of the villa, and I start to walk her in that direction.

"I am from Georgia," I say, "the country that shares the name of your state."

"How do you know where I'm from?" she says, eyes widening in surprise, but I wave her off.

"All of you girls, you put your lives up on display on the internet for all to see. It was easy to find you. I know where you are from, what school you went to, and your impressive cheerleading career-"

"You *stalked* us!" she says, and I raise my eyebrows in genuine surprise.

"We kidnapped you, *chemo kargo*," I say with a smile. "Do you think we would do such a thing without adequate preparation?"

She falls silent for a few moments, chewing her lip as we walk. I look back at her and catch her watching me, curiosity in her eyes.

"Georgia," she says, furrowing her brow. "That's where the war with Russia was a few years ago, wasn't it?"

"Ah, so you know *of* it," I say, grinning as my eyes watch the sand in front of me for a few moments, leading Delaney along. "Do you know how strange it is to hear someone talk of your homeland like some strange place in the corners of the public eye?"

"And I suppose you're going to blame me for that?" she says, and this time, I pull her forward roughly, right up to my chest as I turn around and face her, looming over her in the moonlight. My eyes bore into hers as her breath catches in her throat, and I feel her start to shake in my grip as I watch her carefully.

"This war," I say bitterly, "this footnote in American media — when I was released from prison, that war became my life. My friends and I, some of them my associates today, we were thrust out into the war right out of prison. It was all we had to look forward to."

I bring my fingers to the hem of her dress, running them along it slowly, taking in the feel of the fabric. I bring my hand up to the back of the dress, doing the same there, my fingers brushing against her skin. Her cheeks redden as she watches me, listening.

"You're eighteen. While you use this time to celebrate with friends, put your memories up for the world to see, prance around Europe in expensive dresses, flirt with men from around the world — when we were eighteen, we were sent to become faceless casualties in a war we were goaded into. We were given nothing, and we had nothing to look forward to. Nothing the law would give us, anyway," I add, twirling one of her locks of hair around my finger with a smile. For the first time, she doesn't pull away from me or look terrified.

"You like this, don't you?" she says, her voice

barely more than a whisper. "Making money off people like me."

"A man must take pride in his work," I say, turning and tugging her along with me. "Besides, a little hardship might be good for you. Nobody should live their life like they have the whole world at their feet without being brought down into it once in a while. But tell me," I ask, suddenly pulling her up to my side and wrapping my arm around her waist, smiling down on her as if she were my date once again, "since we're on this romantic walk of ours, why don't you tell me about your life in the stars?"

Her face flushes again when I yank her forward, taking her in beside me. The look in her eyes is unmistakable, and it fills my heart with fire. She's not used to this, getting ordered around and forced to obey commands. Better yet, she likes it. I could take her right now, if I wanted — strip that fancy dress off her and have her riding my cock right here on the Spanish shore, and all I would have to do is keep pushing her just a little further.

"I...wasn't exactly the center of attention all my life," she says after a few moments of silence, slowly, her eyes moving reluctantly from me out onto the waters. "I probably can't compare to, you know, Georgian prison and a war against Russia, but..." she raised her eyebrows a moment, thoughtful. "I guess you could say I've had to adapt. I didn't focus on my looks or how to talk to people that much when I was really young, and I learned pretty quickly that you can't do that as a girl." There is a hint of ruefulness in her voice, but only an undertone, and I glance at her, interested.

"Oh?"

"Boys will tear you apart if you don't look or act a certain way," she says, chewing her lip a moment. "Girls will too, but mostly because their dads taught them to."

"And what did your daddy teach *you*?" I ask, and she turns her big blue eyes up to me before rolling them.

"*My* dad? I could get whatever I want from him. I learned how to 'walk the walk' on my own. I had to," she says, and I can see a hint of confidence in the statement. I find myself smiling, looking down at her, and she catches me a moment later, furrowing her brow over those eyes I could look into for ages.

"What? What is it?"

My hand squeezes her closer to me. "Nothing. Enjoy the walk, Delaney. It's not much farther to the villa now." I flash her a grin. "You ought to enjoy your time at the beach while it lasts.

Half an hour later, we reach the point where I have to take her back up off the beach to march up to the compound. As we start to leave behind the sand, she yelps as I sweep her off her feet, carrying her over the forest floor as we make our way to the cliffs. She squirms in my grip, surprised, but in time, she finds it more comfortable to put her arms around my neck for support, though she seems reluctant to do so at first.

She's tired by the time I step up to the villa entrance, where two of the guards hail me with grinning faces and a wave, but she fights off sleep the whole way.

I find myself impressed by the girl's resilience. Most people would be exhausted after such an escape attempt and the rush of being recaptured, but Delaney fights through it, keeping her eyes alert around her.

I carry her up the stairs, back to her room. This time of night, there are few people around the halls walking about. Nobody questions me as I take her in, but one of the guards, a man with a thick face and ugly brow follows us to the room, nodding to me and closing the door behind us as I head inside and set Delaney down on the bed. I glance over to the window to notice that it's been boarded up from the outside, and I smirk at Delaney, who makes a pouty face.

"Like I'd try it again," she says in a huff.

"Nobody expects lightning to strike in the same place twice, little girl," I say, but there's a warning to my tone, and instead of stepping away from the bed, I stand there as she looks up at me defiantly, crossing her arms.

"Now what are you not going to do again?" I ask, my tone condescendingly chiding as I look down at her with a smile, and she frowns, refusing to speak. "I want to hear you promise me," I say in a lower tone, leaning down at taking her chin in my thumb and forefinger to look at her with a piercing gaze. She blushes, holding back for a few moments more, and I narrow my eyes.

"Let me make something clear, doll," I say, putting my knee on the other side of her, leaning into her and forcing her to lean back, her face reddening even more as I take one of her hands at the wrist and press it into the pillow behind her as she lays back on it, my body nearly horizontal over her. "I've been kind to you tonight in bringing you back, but I don't want you to make the mistake of thinking you're anything more than a case of money to me. You aren't with your daddy anymore," I growl into her ear, and I can practically hear her heart racing. "You are my prisoner. And I *will* get what I want from you. You have more spirit than most, I'll give you that, but if you don't behave, I'll be all the more tempted to keep you here for myself, you pretty little brat." I raise my head, looking down at her wide, petrified eyes.

"I promise," she breathes, her body trembling with both fear and need under my looming, rock-hard form. "I promise, Darios, I won't try to escape again."

"That's a good girl," I say, rising up again and lingering a moment before standing and bringing the bedsheets over her body, tucking her in. I turn and head for the door, my face stony as I stride away from her, feeling her eyes on my back. "Sweet dreams, Delaney."

I open the door, and my guard jumps back, a surprised look on his face. He must have been listening I give him a hard look as I shut the door behind me, then lock it. I start to head down the hall, but I cast a glance over my shoulder after about twenty paces.

The guard is looking at the door with a hungry look in his eyes. A moment later, he looks up and meets my gaze, blanches, then walks in the opposite direction, disappearing behind a corner. I frown.

I'll need to watch that one carefully. He gives me a bad feeling.

I sit on the edge of my bed, staring at the stained, aged walls and trying not to think about the fact that my escape was so poorly executed. I am not accustomed to failure, and I'm finding it to be an excessively uncomfortable feeling. Especially once Darios showed me just how close I had been to potential safety, the Mediterranean coastline just beyond my grasp. I feel like such a fool, thinking I could simply throw myself out a window into the dark, wild night with no sense of direction or further plan and actually survive. I am a very smart girl, I know that without a doubt, but I've always been more apt to plan everything down to each detail rather than to just dive in spontaneously. I don't like winging it. That's never been my forte.

But desperate times do call for desperate measures, I remind myself calmly. And it didn't go as badly as it could have gone. I wasn't eaten by a wolf. I didn't fall into a sinkhole and break my legs. And Darios, upon catching up to me as he inevitably would, did not kill me for my transgression.

I bite my lip and look down at my empty palm, remembering the sensation of Darios's hand taking mine, his fingers completely encapsulating my much smaller, daintier hand. A shiver runs involuntarily through my body and I sigh, rolling my eyes to the heavens at my own physical response. Am I really so lonely and desperate that I am beginning to have fond feelings for the very man who has made my life hell? A jolt of discomfort racks my brain; am I experiencing Stockholm Syndrome?

"No, come on. You're better than this. Get yourself together," I murmur softly to myself, shutting my eyes tightly. "Delaney Underwood does not get the softy-feelies for her captor. Get a grip."

But the feeling remains, like a tiny voice whispering in the back of my head, prodding me to explore the question further: how do I really feel about Darios?

"Nope," I mumble firmly, getting to my feet and pacing back and forth across the little room. I shouldn't be thinking about this at all. I should be busy trying to figure out my next move. I should be concocting a new plan, a new strategy for saving my own ass. And I should be doing everything I can to rescue my friends. Megan may have been lucky enough to go home with her family, but to my knowledge, Lyssa and Caitlin are still being held against their will, too. Just like me.

I gulp. *Or worse.*

For all I know, they could have it even worse than I do. In fact, I have not seen or heard anything about either of them since we first got shoved into separate cells. I don't know if they're alive or dead. My stomach churns and bile rises in my throat at the thought of two of my best friends being hurt or threatened by these wolfish predators. I have to swallow hard and fan myself a little bit to tame the nausea in my gut, my heart pounding in my chest.

I have done my best not to think about the worst possible scenarios so far, because dwelling on the negatives has never really done much to help in the past. I find that I focus best when I can make myself a little detached from a situation. I have to remove my emotions entirely and just thinking as logically as possible. But this time, I can feel the tsunami waves of emotion starting to build height and power in my heart, and I don't know if I can stave off my feelings.

As much as I try to play the cool girl, I can't deny that I really, truly love my friends. I cannot stand the idea of anything terrible befalling them — especially because it would be my fault. I brought them here. It was my own arrogance that deceived the four of us into thinking we could just fly to another country and live out some *Sex and the City* fantasy. I rack my brain, trying to think critically about our predicament.

Megan is safe. At least I don't have to worry about her anymore.

Lyssa is probably okay, since she is both smart enough and soft-spoken enough to stay out of the men's way. She knows when to shut up and go with the flow when necessary. So unless one of the men has simply decided to indulge a sadistic streak or something, I'm fairly certain Lyssa has managed to evade the worst of it.

But Caitlin... she is the one to worry about. My best friend is both sassy and forward, and her sarcastic, biting wit has launched her into hot water many times in the past. She's the one who always says what's on her mind, who isn't afraid to step on people's toes — or even their heads — to get what she wants. I've seen her throw fits at restaurants when the waiter doesn't refill her drink fast enough. She's a hothead, and I know that kind of temper probably isn't doing her any favors right now.

And I'm not even sure her parents can afford the ransom. I haven't told any of our friends, or her, but I have a hunch that her family isn't as well off as she pretends she is.

Hopefully she has figured out how to be quiet and stay out of the way since we've arrived here, but something tells me it would take something truly monumental to make her change her ways. Although, to be fair, being kidnapped and held for ransom in a dilapidated Spanish villa by a group of murderous Georgian mobsters should probably qualify as a monumental life event.

There's a knock on my door and I swivel around instantly, being ripped out of my thoughts. Darios steps inside, holding a large bottle of water and a plate of bread and grapes. He lifts these objects up a little, giving me a questioning glare.

"What is this?" I ask a little suspiciously, folding my arms over my chest. "Poisoned food?"

Darios laughs and shakes his head. "If I wanted to kill you, do you really think I would waste a perfectly good meal to do it? Besides, you should know by now that you are more valuable to me alive than dead."

"Oh, that's reassuring. Thank you," I reply, but to my frustration I feel just a hint of a smile trying to form on my lips. What the hell is wrong with me? A smile is not an appropriate response to a very thinly veiled threat on my life.

"Come. Eat. And tell me more about yourself. I am interested in hearing about your life, especially since you are so keen to preserve it," he urges me, setting the plate down on the bed, patting the spot next to it expectantly. With a reluctant sigh I walk over and sit down. My stomach growls loudly, betraying the fact that I really, really do want to eat this food. Darios smiles as I begin to rip off bits of the thick, fluffy bread and eat. Immediately I am awash in grateful warmth, not realizing until now just how ravenously hungry I am.

"Well, I don't know what else about my life you even need to know, since you've already stalked me on social media, apparently," I quip. Darios simply stares at me, not bothered by my remark. "Fine. What do you want to know?"

"You seem different from the girl depicted on your accounts," he begins slowly. "The Delaney Underwood who posts photos of her outfits and coffee drinks does not suit this version of you."

"This version of me isn't exactly living the same life anymore, thanks to you," I reply sharply.

"I prefer this version," Darios says, and I hate myself for blushing. I want to be angry, not flattered. I pop a grape into my mouth and shrug callously.

"I don't care what you like," I shoot back, but the look he gives me makes my skin crawl.

Darios leans in and whispers, "Yes, you do."

I freeze for a moment, every cell in my body paralyzed with — what? Fear? Anger? Desire?

"Besides," he continues, resuming his former cold nonchalance, "I believe that this is more like the real you, anyway. Nobody knows what they are truly made of until they are taken out of their element and broken down."

"Wonderful. So all of this is just one big social experiment for me to 'find myself' or whatever?"

Darios grins. "If it pleases you to think of it that way, then so be it. It certainly seems to me that you are more clever than you let on. You are stronger than you want people to think you are. And you must admit, this experience is showing you more about who you really are than your easy, shallow life back home."

"It's not my fault everyone underestimates me," I say softly, clenching my jaw. Darios reaches out and takes my chin between his fingers, his thumb tracing over my bottom lip.

Gazing powerfully into my eyes, he says, "They see exactly what you allow them to see. You give them no reason to believe otherwise. When was the last time you really worked hard for anything?"

Indignant fury bubbles in my chest as I spit out a reply. "Cheerleading."

"Yes, and were you good at it?"

"I was the best."

"And then what happened?"

I pause, not wanting to answer. But he prods me onward with a glance and I mumble, "And then I quit the squad."

Darios releases me and stands back up, walking across the room to the door. "Exactly," he says shortly. He winks at me and heads out into the hall-way, his footsteps thudding faintly away.

I'm left sitting alone in my room, my appetite entirely gone thanks to our sour exchange. I hate being disproved. I hate learning that I'm wrong. And I hate the fact that someone like Darios can so easily dissect me and turn me inside out. He doesn't know the real me. Nobody does.

I've made damn sure of that.

As I pick at the food Darios has brought me, I realize that he probably hasn't done this for Lyssa or Caitlin. In fact, Darios has stopped in to see me multiple times a day since we first came here, and if he's spending this much time with me, I find it hard to imagine that he could do the same with anyone else. This realization gives me a tiny thrill, which I immediately resent. I can't believe how quickly he has gotten under my skin. It almost feels as though I *want* him to spend more time with me. I hate myself for feeling this way, for wishing deep down that he would come back and talk to me some more. I try to tell myself that it's only a result of being locked away in here by myself. Anyone in this predicament would feel lonely, right?

But I can't pretend it's the same thing. Because instead of longing for the company of my friends, I'm sitting here wishing my dark, dangerous, handsome captor will come back.

How have I suddenly become so deranged? So broken?

As I'm pondering this morbid thought, the door

creaks open again and I glance up, my heart hammering away in my chest. How could Darios have known I've been silently wishing for him to come back in? Can he read my mind or something?

But then my stomach drops when I realize that the man walking in isn't Darios. It's just some other big, burly guard, the one who has been lurking outside my door and bringing me my daily bowl of lumpy gray porridge. Only this time, he's empty-handed.

He shuts and locks the door behind himself, slowly walking over to me with a predatory glint in his black eyes. I back away from him, shaking my head. "Wh-what do you want?" I stammer quietly.

Wordlessly, he bolts forward and in one swift motion he grasps me by the wrists, tugging me closer to him. I open my mouth to scream but he claps a hand over my lips, strangling the cry in my throat as he slams me back into the stony wall. "*Mshvidad iqavi,*" he hisses in a low voice.

He thrusts a knee between my legs, prying my thighs apart despite my attempts to struggle free, a cruel smirk on his face. "If you scream, I will bash your head in," he growls as he releases my mouth to reach down between my thighs. Despite his threat, I immediately fill my lungs with air and scream.

The man wraps both hands around my throat and throws me down to the floor, pinning me with his enormous weight so that the breath is knocked out of my body entirely. "I told you to shut up," he sneers furiously. As I struggle to breathe with his thumb pressed hard against my windpipe, he unbuttons his trousers and I begin to kick wildly.

Just as the man pulls his fist back in preparation to strike me, there's the jostle of a key in the door and then it bursts open. My eyesight is starting to go dark while someone — some powerful force — rips the man off of me. I gasp for breath, coughing as I force myself into a sitting position and look around. As my vision clears, I realize with a jolt that the man who came in to save me is Darios. He's knocked my would-be assailant to the floor and is pummeling his face with brutal blows, blood streaking his knuckles with each strike.

"*Nabozvaro!*" Darios bellows, strangling the man with both hands. "Filthy dog!"

The man's eyes are bulging out of his head, his fingers scrambling helplessly to peel Darios's hands off his throat, and I realize that if I don't intervene, I may be about to watch a man die.

"Darios! Stop!" I try to yelp, still too paralyzed with shock to move. But my voice is weak, and Darios does not listen. I watch in mingled horror and gratitude as he pulls the man to a standing position and walks him backward to the window. I cannot move or even breathe as I watch Darios pull away the thin sheet which has been covering the window and kicks the man through the opening with enough force to violently shatter the wooden barricade. I let out a breathless shriek as my attacker falls to his death.

I can feel my entire body tingling, almost numb with shock as I somehow get myself to my feet and walk over to Darios, who is still standing by the window. I can feel his dark, blazing eyes on me as I approach, watching me. Wondering how I will react.

The truth is, I have no idea what I'm feeling, beyond a rush of morbid gratitude. Darios has saved me, yet again, from an absolutely dismal fate. I press myself into his hard, daunting frame, all but collapsing into his arms. He catches me, a flash of surprise on his face as I look up at him.

There is a still, silent moment in which the world around us melts away. Every sight, sound, and smell of the holding cell disappears. All that remains is the small, empty space between us. Without a second thought, without hesitation, I lurch forward and wrap my arms around him just as he bends to meet my lips in a biting, desperate kiss.

Adrenaline flooding my veins, I rip away from him just long enough to tear my dress up and over my head, casting it across the room. There are no thoughts behind my actions, no consideration for consequences. I'm filled with almost an animalistic need, and one glance at my captor tells me he's in the same state.

Darios strips out of his shirt and frantically

unbuttons his trousers, stepping out of them and pressing into me. He's tall and broad, towering over me, and I can see the raising of his chest with his deep breaths, but he doesn't touch me. His presence is enough, and I can feel it all over me as I shrug my bra off down to the floor, leaving me standing totally naked and exposed before this man.

This *murderer*.

His hands finally reach out and rove down my vulnerable, soft body with a hunger and ferocity that stirs something raw deep within myself, something I've never felt in all my life. I lean into his touch greedily, wanting him to run his fingers down every inch of my virgin flesh. I want him to mark me. Make me his.

I want him to ruin me.

Without a single word, he lifts me up and carries me to the bed, knocking the plate of food haphazardly to the floor with a loud clatter to make room. Darios wrenches my thighs open and I suck in a sharp breath, both terrified and impatient for him to make his next move. Looking up at me with his dark eyes smoldering, he plunges a finger inside of me with no warning, no preamble whatsoever. I shout out and buck into the pressure, having never had any part of another person inside me before. Darios stands up and crawls over me, nipping and sucking at my breasts while his finger works into me deeper and deeper. Just as I can feel myself building toward a powerful, indescribable peak, he withdraws his finger, raising it to his lips and sucking my own juices into his mouth.

He kisses me hard while he deftly removes his tight, black briefs, and his cock springs free, brushing against my thigh. Unable to stop myself, I reach down to grip his enormous, thick shaft in my hand, and I gasp at the surprising size. Darios groans and pushes into my hand for a moment, then pins both of my arms down above my head.

With his other hand he guides the head of his shaft to my slick, shuddering hole, then pushes inside. I cry out as a flash of horrible pain seizes my body. It feels as though Darios is splitting me in two, cleaving me straight down the middle! It feels like my insides are shattering. Darios is breaking me down and destroying me, utterly, but I want him to.

I need him to.

Quickly, he begins to thrust into me without any regard for my pain, his lips grazing my sensitive nipples, my panting mouth, my exposed neck. As he pumps into me fast and hard, I feel my own pain starting to give way to a new, shocking pleasure. I rock upward to meet his thrusts, clawing desperately at his back as I whimper his name over and over, starting to fully lose myself in the overwhelming combination of bliss and agony. Grasping the headboard to get better control, Darios straightens up and pulls my legs up over his shoulder, my ankles hooked around his neck. I feel my former flexibility as a cheerleader showing through, and the look on Darios's face when I use this new position to roll my hips into him gives me a thrill of filthy delight. To reward me, he uses two fingers to stroke my clit in a circular motion as he thrusts into me, and my pleasure mounts higher and higher until I cry out, my climax bursting over me in an almost painful rush.

Darios groans his satisfaction at having brought me to orgasm, his rhythm becoming faster and more erratic until finally he shoves deep within me and releases a hot stream of seed. He bellows my name and bends to kiss me, his tongue forcing its way into my mouth as I feel his cream pumping into my cunt.

As we breathe raggedly against each other in the hot, sticky air, I murmur, "Promise me you will protect me. Promise me…"

"You are mine," he growls, his forehead pressed against mine. "And I will always guard what belongs to me."

He stands up, dresses quickly, then stalks out of the room without another word, leaving me to lie breathless and stunned on the bed with his seed slowly leaking out of me onto the sheets. I stare up at the ceiling, one thought piercing sharply through the fog of shock and confusion in my mind.

Have I fallen in love with my captor?

DARIOS

I wonder if the police find stakeouts this tedious.

I'm sitting in my car, engine off, across the street and down the block from the apartment of a small, well-to-do family who lives in the high-rise on the corner of the street. The father is a travel agent working for one of the top companies in the country, and the mother is an aerospace engineer working for a small non-profit.

And their daughter earned us several million in cash last year in ransom money.

I thumb to the next page on the Kindle I'm holding in my hands, re-reading some old mystery novel I bought to kill time for stakeouts like this. It also gives me a decent cover — few in Spain should mind a well-dressed man reading alone in his car.

I'm out here tonight because I know the father's routine will soon have him walk out of his apartment, from where he'll head two blocks down to the corner store to buy cigarettes. He knows his wife and daughter don't approve of his habit, so he's already self-conscious and jumpy on the way there. He lives in a safe part of Barcelona, though, so he'll not be glancing over his shoulders for fear of petty criminals. I couldn't have him in a better position.

There's nothing wrong with him as a person, in the grand scheme of things, but I always keep track of my former clients, and I often entrust only myself with the task of these little follow-up visits I choose to conduct.

When our ransom victims are safely in our grasp, we almost never have trouble with the parents going to the police. We're highly selective of those we choose to abduct, looking for parents who are more apt to panic than to take decisive action against us. And those who do act often find their connections bribed or threatened into silence. I've gone so far as to show up at the houses of government officials with firm warnings.

I feel no remorse for my actions. These people wallow in the lap of luxury all their lives, while those under them, sometimes their direct subordinates, suffer on a daily basis. I'm only leveling the playing field however I can, and I make a little money while

I'm doing it. This is my operation, and I won't see it threatened by any heroics.

So I come by to visit the parents of past hostages to say 'hello' and make sure they're still keeping our business arrangements quiet. Once the money has changed hands, it's much more likely for the parents to try to go to the media or the police and try to expose our operation. Of course, many of them do so well aware that we continue to keep hostages, but I doubt they care much for the well-being of other girls. As long as *their* precious princess is safe and sound, the others couldn't matter less to them.

This is why we target groups of friends. If the parents know each other, it's more likely they'll cooperate and not go to the police the moment their daughter is safe — it would make for awkward dinner conversations if one family's carelessness was directly responsible for another's loss of a daughter.

And the media is always dying for the chance to make a circus out of a hostage situation like ours. I suspect rumors have gotten out in the past, so the news outlets keep ears out for us like some mysterious white whale, and the police are getting more and more willing to collaborate with them in the hopes of putting a stop to the threat to tourism we represent.

In all honesty, making the media, the police, and tourists lie awake in their beds at night in one fell swoop gives me a sense of quiet satisfaction. I don't plan to do the people I check up on any harm, unless their actions demand it. The mere fact of my ability to track these people is usually enough to scare them into silence.

They know I won't hesitate to take their daughters again.

As I glance up at the apartment again, I catch a whiff of Delaney's perfume, her scent still on my body after the moments of passion we shared earlier today. I feel a smile come across my features despite myself, and I lower the Kindle a moment, realizing that I'm just glazing over the words while the fresh memory of her occupies my thoughts and makes my cock start to stiffen again, so soon after being spent.

When I first hauled Delaney into the van, I hadn't expected anything like this to happen, but the more time that spoiled brat spends around me, the more I want to fuck her until she's exhausted, her tight cunt hugging my cock while she begs for more.

And she will.

She's an interesting girl. There's a real power of observation in that head of golden hair, a sharpness I hadn't anticipated when I took her. She's either ignored her potential all her life or willingly covered it up under a veneer of cheerleading, parties, and flashy clothes. Maybe I ought to rip those expensive outfits off her while I show her what she can really do under it all.

I give my head a light shake, reminding myself that she's just another hostage — just another daddy's princess waiting to be rescued by his money, the only thing it sounds like Delaney's father knows how to use. I find myself smiling again, pretending to re-read the page I'm on for the fourth time. I would be surprised if I'll ever find a man quite as pliable and spineless as Delaney's father. When we first reached out to him, he was nearly incoherent at the thought of his precious little girl being in danger.

And from what Delaney said, it sounds like she picks up on her father's weakness, too. Small wonder the girl is so bored, with such a pitiful man in her life. It makes me want to follow through with my threat of keeping her for myself all the more.

And what if I do?

That's a thought that's crossed my mind a few times. I wonder what the look on her face would be if I told her I'd settled on that? I smile. The way she's been acting, she might well like the idea.

She's desperate for me. The feeling of her wet pussy on my cock earlier told me all I needed to know about that, and I'm going to get so much more out of her before I'm done with her.

I find myself wondering what her upbringing must feel like, to be surrounded by people whose only motivation in life is the things money can afford her. No wonder she finds herself surrounding herself with trinkets and idle pastimes — it's all she's been taught her whole life. I grunt, frustrated with myself. Why do I find myself sympathizing a little with this spoiled American? She's basked in the lap of luxury all her life. But that just makes me want to fuck her harder until she begs for something *real* in her life, a cock that can't be bought with money.

Before my cock gets harder, I'm snapped out of my thoughts by the sight of the door opening and the father of my old victim heading out, about five minutes late of schedule. I let him get a few paces before I open my car door and start to follow him, silently. The streets of Barcelona are usually bustling with activity, but in this part of town, an upscale neighborhood that rich locals and expats alike envy, it's rare that anything more than a few passing cars disturb the evening's peace.

But even as I tail my man, I can't get the thought of Delaney out of my head. In my mind, I'm grasping her breasts again, shoving my fingers into her sopping cunt and teasing it to do what I please. Maybe I should pay her another visit when I get back, finish the job I started? If she thought that was all I was going to give her, she'd made a terrible mistake.

I'm so wrapped up in my thoughts that I almost make a sound as I gain ground on my target. But I catch myself, and just as he's about to cross a street, I step up to his side, smiling at him as if he were an old friend I'd just caught up with.

"Good to see you again, Señor Gonzalez," I greet him in Spanish, and he does a double-take at me, his eyes widening as he realizes who I am. I watch his face pale and his hands start to shake immediately. "Keep your eyes forward, we're having a friendly conversation," I say in a low tone, and he complies like an obedient dog, bobbing his head.

"We paid," he replies quietly, his voice hoarse, but I give him a pained smile and narrow my eyes.

"That doesn't sound like a friendly conversation, Señor Gonzalez. So tell me," I say, raising my voice to a normal speaking tone, "how is the family these days?"

He walks with me a few paces before finding his voice, strained to keep it level. "Very well," he says, "my wife j-just got a promotion. I'm very proud of her."

"Ah, I can imagine — she must be a sharp woman to be doing as well in this economy as she is!"

"Yes."

"And I presume your daughter is taking after her swimmingly? I hear she's joining the journalism club at her university."

The man looks at me with fear in his eyes, and I smile cordially back at him. My knowledge of his daughter's movements seems to have spooked him. I can't blame him — few of my clients think about the fact that I keep track of the whole family after our business is concluded.

"You ought to tell her she should be careful, running with the journalist crowd," I say meaningfully. "They're prone to gossip. Friends who talk fast and loose around the media can be dangerous at best. Attract unwanted attention. At least, most concerned fathers would think so."

He stares at me in disbelief, but I can see that he's understood my message perfectly, and I grin, patting him on the back as we walk.

"I'm only looking out for you, my friend. You never know what kind of trouble a girl can get into on campus, even from something as simple as chatting with the campus police," I add, shooting him another look.

The man seems on the verge of tears, and finally, I gently lead him into an alley where we can talk in privacy, and immediately, thinking his life in danger, he breaks down in front of me.

"I swear, we haven't betrayed our silence, sir," he whimpers without my even bothering to take out a gun. "But you should know — the police, they have asked questions. We got a call not long ago, someone claiming the department is asking for locals to report 'suspicious activity' in the area."

"Oh?" I say, raising an interested eyebrow. This, I don't know about. He nods fiercely.

"But when I asked my neighbors about the call, none of them say they've received it. I think they called us alone. But I swear to you, we'd never breathe a word — we're eternally grateful for how well you treated our daughter! She'd be dead if you hadn't been guiding the whole thing — thank you, sir, thank you!"

"Enough whimpering," I scold the man, bored by his near-groveling. "Good of you to tell me this, though."

This is troubling news. If the police are asking questions, then that means there's been a leak, and they're on our trail. If it was Sandro, then that problem has already been taken care of, but there's no way of knowing if he was the only traitor. Suddenly I regret finishing him off without torturing him for information first. How far have they gotten? What other people have they reached out to? I'm going to have to make a lot of visits in a short amount of time, it seems. I cannot risk the police getting involved at this stage of my game. The media will tear it apart, leaving us no breathing room to continue.

"Of course, sir," he says, bobbing his head again.

"Now take a walk around the block before you get your cigarettes, Señor Gonzalez," I say, putting on my fake smile again. "You'll want to clear your head before going back to your family — oh, and tell your wife her new teal dress suits her well," I add, and he swallows hard, nodding.

"Of course. We're in your debt, sir."

"Remember that, Señor Gonzalez," I say as I start to walk off, looking at him over my shoulder with a kind smile and speaking casually. "If you don't, I'll have one of those hands of yours sent to your mother in a shoebox."

I suck in a long, deep breath and carefully lie back onto the stony roof terrace, staring up at the silky black sky speckled with constellations. The stars are bright and stunning this evening, and since Darios has been gone for hours and hours, I've gotten bored enough to venture out — at great risk. I've been trapped in the villa long enough with nothing to distract me that I have taken to memorizing the guards' routines.

Even without an actual clock to go by, I am learning how to track the passage of time, if only roughly, simply by watching the rising and falling dance of the sun and moon. I know what times the guards come and go, how long each individual man spends at the post outside my door. They very rarely check in on me, choosing to just stand outside. Probably because they know I'm very unlikely to try and escape again after my first spectacular failure.

But one thing I have done is lean as far out the window as I can manage without falling, squinting up at the building. There is an old column near my window which has been whittled away over the course of many decades, and I have been eyeing it for a while now, sizing up the chunks missing out of its circular trunk. I determined that it looked at least somewhat climbable — enough to hoist myself out the window and up the column to pull myself onto the mostly-flat roof of the villa.

It was obviously a very dangerous choice, but it was one I do not regret. In fact, I am finding that I rather enjoy taking big risks lately. In particular, my decision to give up my virginity to Darios was a bit of a leap from my usual prudishness. I've guarded my purity for so long, not allowing anyone past the fortress I've built around myself. It's safer to keep the walls up. It's better to keep people standing on tiptoe to catch a glimpse of your greatness, the shining light behind the curtain. I always believed that once I gave in to what every man wanted from me, I would lose some of that shine. Every book, movie, and television show I encountered only reinforced that belief.

From what I have seen, people — especially men — only want what they can't have. And once you give them what they ask for, they're done with you.

I always assumed my first time would be magical and romantic. Flickering candles, soft music, and gentle kisses. Boys tend to put girls like me high up on unreachable pedestals, pouring all their loftiest expectations into us. Brandon looked at me like I was something simultaneously fragile and consumable. He was always asking for permission to kiss me, pressuring me to go further, his hands trembling as he reached to unclasp my bra.

I always stopped him.

"It's just not the right time," I would tell him, shrugging apologetically as I pulled my cardigan back on. He would fix me with that doleful stare, the telltale muscle in his jaw twitching as he tried to calm himself down and act nonchalant. But I knew it killed him every time, just a little bit, to have me rip the gift right back out of his hands. And I'm sure he thought I was just doing it to tease him. Perhaps there was a part of me who did it for that reason. But overwhelmingly, it was because I was scared that once he got what he wanted from me… he would leave. I was afraid to give my power to anyone else.

Brandon was insistent. And *per*sistent. He tried everything — sweet talk, bribery, guilt tripping. He begged me and promised me the world some days, and other days he would threaten to leave me for someone who would "give into his love." Those days generally culminated in a huge fight, at the end of which he would chase me out into the street spouting off a string of insincere apologies. He would then swear to me, "Delaney, I promise I won't ever try to push you into something you don't want to do," only to start the whole cycle over again the next day.

He just couldn't let it go, no matter how many excuses I gave him. For years, it felt like we were participating in some slow-motion tug of war, with a mattress in the middle. He pulled from one side, trying to rope me into sleeping with him, but I just kept pulling my own weight.

Fighting back. Constantly.

It was incredibly tiring, and it cemented my suspicion that the only thing men would ever value in me is my sexuality. Well, that or my ability to stroke their ego in other ways. My father, for example, spoils me like mad, but only because I bat my eyelashes at him and rush to his arms to tell him about my vapid daily life. I greet him with a big smile when he comes home from work. I bake him cookies to take to the office. I basically play the role of a trophy-wife-in-training, and I do it well. I make him feel like he's the best father in the world, like everything I do is an effort to make him proud of me. Sure, he does want me to succeed, but just so that he has the bragging rights to tell his pervy old friends at the country club that his daughter is a pretty, popular prom queen. I always suspected that those same old guys would go home to their Georgia mansions and think about me in bed.

In fact, I pretty much assume that every man I meet is just hoping for the opportunity to get me naked and take something away from me. I have to stay vigilant and guard my most precious gift. Keeping up with the chase is exhausting, but I've had to do it for all these years.

Until now.

I sigh, blinking up at the glorious night sky above me, feeling a little lost. What kind of woman am I shaping up to be if the first man I give myself to is also my murderous, dangerous captor? What does it say about me that I lost my virginity directly after watching him push a man through a high window? Of course, it does make me feel slightly relieved to remember that Darios did save my life. The man who was trying to take advantage of me... he could have killed me. Easily. Darios stepped in and took my side without a moment's hesitation. He could have simply let his guard carry on and do what he wanted with me. But he didn't.

Perhaps it was only fitting that his ultimate act of bravery be rewarded with my near-ultimate act of sacrifice. He saved my life, so I gave him my body.

I shudder to myself, closing my eyes and reliving the hot touch of Darios's hands grasping at me possessively, maneuvering me around like I was a feather-light doll or something. He handled me like I belonged to him, like he knew exactly what I wanted him to do.

Like he'd thought about it many times before.

I lick my lips, letting my hands wander down my body and between my thighs, slowly pulling up the hem of my black dress. Strangely enough, out here on the roof in the open air, I have the most privacy I've enjoyed in a long time. Even when I bathe in the one working bathtub in the little round room down the hall from my cell, two guards stand by to keep watch. Obviously I insist on having them look away... and they don't listen. As if I could possibly escape while naked in a bathtub.

But now, nobody is around to gawk at me. To look me up and down like hungry animals. I'm finally alone, at least for a little while. I close my eyes and begin to gently, tentatively stroke my dampening slit, feeling every nerve in my body flutter to life under the stars. I begin to move my hips ever so slightly with the rhythm of my fingers, my lips parting to emit a soft gasp.

And then I'm interrupted by the sensation of something — or someone — grabbing hold of my shoulders. My eyes fly open to reveal the shadowy outline of Darios's face, hovering over me wearing a cruel smirk. Immediately embarrassed, I try to struggle out of his grasp, hastily shoving my dress back down over my thighs. But he catches me in his arms and pulls me close, breathing roughly in my ear.

"I thought you promised not to sneak out again, little girl," he growls, sending a shiver down my spine. His fingers brush across my neck and I gulp.

"I wasn't trying to run away or anything," I explain quickly, my body tensing up with mingled fear and desire. I can feel the smooth, hard shape of his cock against my back as he pulls me into his lap, gazing down at my face. "I-I just wanted a little privacy."

"Oh, I can see that," Darios says, one of his hands trailing down to dip between my thighs. I let out a startled whimper and close my legs tightly, but he only laughs. "Did you really come all the way up here just to be alone?"

I nod. "Y-Yes, I just needed to get some time for myself. The men — they're always watching me, and I—"

"— and you wanted a place where nobody could see you touch yourself," he interrupts, clucking his tongue in faux pity. "You filthy little bird. Didn't I give you more than enough the first time?"

I can't even manage to choke out a single word in response. I can't remember the last time I was ever truly speechless, but right now, I definitely am. Darios deftly hoists my dress up to my hips to give himself a better view of my thighs and pussy. I hold my breath involuntarily as he reaches down and starts to softly stroke my clit in a circular design. I arch my back and lean into him limply, feeling every part of my body fall to mush in his arms. The walls I have built so tall and strong around my heart, around my sexuality, are crumbling in heavy piles around me.

It blows my mind that Darios, this hulking, dangerous criminal of a man, can so effortlessly strip away all my best defenses. He can break me down and split me asunder with just a simple touch.

"That's my good girl," he whispers in my ear. His warm breath on my neck makes me shiver in ticklish delight and he laughs, starting to quicken his circling of my clit until I'm writhing in his arms, gasping for release. This time he doesn't pull away just short of the finish line — he ever so gently pinches my clit between his thumb and forefinger at just the right moment and I cry out, my body shuddering with a long-awaited climax.

"Ahh, Darios!" I breathe, my chest heaving. He cups my pulsing mound, holding me through the trembles of my orgasm even as his other hand slides down inside the bustline of my dress, slipping down to caress my breasts. I am nothing more than modeling clay in his hands, my every insecurity and worry retreating into the shadows, to emerge at a later time when I'm alone. For now, I belong to Darios, and nothing can distract me from the sensation of his hands roving down my body.

He murmurs something in his native tongue that I can't understand, speaking more to himself than to me. "*Ghmerto chemo,*" he mumbles, flicking his thumb across my stiffening nipples. I push upward into his palm and he looks down at me with an almost tender gaze. But the softness fades immediately to be replaced by a mischievous grin. He pulls me up into a kneeling position so that I'm resting upright on my knees, then leans in to kiss me passionately, his tongue pushing into my mouth.

Darios cups my face with both hands for a moment, his fingers tracing along the swell of my cheek and the curve of my jaw, then smoothing the hair back from my temples to tuck behind my ear. This fond gesture is cut short when he reaches around to grab a fistful of my hair, jerking my head back so that more of my neck is exposed. He quickly dives forward to suck a bruising, tantalizing kiss into my bare shoulder. The sensation is almost painful, but it feels nearly orgasmic in itself at the same time. He kisses a line down to my chest, where he pauses a moment to pull my dress up over my head and drop it to the side. For a moment I panic, both at the thought of being totally naked on a rooftop with a serial murderer and because I worry that my dress might blow off into the wind.

But I don't get much time to worry, as Darios hastily wrenches me forward, forcing me to catch myself on my palms. There's a flash of wild desire in his eyes and he groans his pleasure at the sight of me kneeling on all fours in front of him. Instantly he gets up and walks around behind me, evidently not even the least bit worried about possibly falling off the roof. It's pretty sturdy and horizontal, but I still would not want to risk standing up all the way just in case my center of gravity is thrown off-kilter.

However, Darios has entirely different thoughts on his mind.

Positioning himself behind me, he reaches around to grab my hips, maneuvering me backward so that my ass grinds against the hard outline of his cock through his trousers. He groans his appreciation and I hear the faint metallic jingle of his belt being removed and his zipper tugged down. I inhale sharply when I feel his enormous, stiffened length pressing against my ass.

"You know I have to punish you for disobeying me," Darios growls, running his hands over my ass cheeks. "You should have known better than to push my limits by coming up here."

"I-I'm sorry," I stammer, hardly able to concentrate with his cock pushed against me. "I wasn't trying to escape — just came up here to get away for a little while."

"Oh yes. 'Privacy.' You wanted to be a dirty girl, so that's exactly what you're going to be."

In the next moment, there's a loud slap as something hard and smooth smacks against my ass. A jolt of pain shoots through my body and I let out a yelp, but Darios only laughs as I look back at him in surprise and confusion. He's holding his leather belt in his hands with a devilish grin on his face.

"How many blows do you think I should give you, Delaney? How severely do you need to be punished, *patara gogona?*" he purrs, landing another smack of the belt. I tremble with pain, but to my surprise and faint horror, I find myself strangely excited by the prospect of receiving further punishment. I'm craving retribution. I'm longing for the pain.

"Answer me, *bavshvi.* How much more do you want?" he continues, sliding the cool leather strip along the outside of my thighs.

"Just a little more, please," I can hear myself murmuring.

"Can you take it?" Darios hisses. "I want to hear you beg for it. Make me punish you."

"Please, Darios. Please... I-I need to p-pay for what I've done," I stammer, still in total disbelief at my own response to such awful treatment.

"Very well," he says, and lands another agonizing strike to my ass, causing me to seize up and gasp in pain even as I feel my pussy dripping with need. Darios drops the belt and slides his hands along the welts forming on my ass cheeks.

His voice is thick and lustful when he says,

"Good girl. You've taken your punishment so well, I think you deserve a reward, don't you?"

"Yes, please," I reply weakly.

And with that, he shoves the head of his erect shaft into my waiting hole, his hands gripping my waist to hold me in place. I cry out and buck backwards into him, feeling the tip of his glorious cock brushing against that deep, special place within me. Darios squeezes my hips and thrusts into me from behind, groaning my name like it's a curse — or a prayer.

I've never been touched this way, so raw and rough and wanting. But Darios slams into me hard, again and again, until we're both gasping for air and barely holding on.

"You love it, don't you, little princess?" Darios growls, quickening his pace. "You love feeling me deep inside your pretty little cunt?"

"Yes! Yes! Oh god, I love it," I'm whimpering, my second orgasm shattering over me.

"*Diakh, bavsvi.* Come for me," he commands in a deep, gravelly tone. I can tell he's beginning to lose control, too, his thrusts becoming deeper and more erratic. "Come for me, Delaney."

And almost like magic, I feel my third climax crash over me like a tidal wave. My elbows buckle and I nearly collapse forward with the rush of uncontrollable pleasure, but Darios holds me still as he continues to slam into my soaking pussy.

With a few frenzied snaps of his hips he clutches hard at my waist and bellows, "Oh *ghmert'i*, Delaney! Fuck!" and he releases his hot seed inside me. He pulls out of me and flips me over, pushing me down onto my back so he can crouch over me. His dark, mysterious eyes survey my trembling body for a moment, and then he leans down to kiss me with a surprising softness.

As he stretches out beside me on the roof, I blink up at the twinkling stars overhead. In the stillness of the moment, I search for the words to say, to fill the vast emptiness surrounding us. But I can only murmur, "It's beautiful out here."

There's a pause, and then Darios begrudgingly replies, "I suppose it is."

I glance over at him in the soft moonlight and see him staring up into the sky, like he's searching for something, some secret message scrawled out in the stars. I wonder what he's thinking. I wonder what he thinks of me.

And even worse… I wonder what I'm beginning to think of him.

DARIOS

This girl is keeping herself in my mind, and I'm getting frustrated that I can't get her out.

I'm striding through the villa, making my way into what used to be a lavish dining room that we now use for storage, occasionally coming back here to smoke or play cards. There are frescoes on the wall — giant murals painted onto the stone that are not nearly as ancient as they're made to look, but the sorry state of the manor enhances the effect of time's ravishing nicely.

It's a remarkably empty room right now, and the only company that seems to haunt me persistently is the fresh thought of Delaney. The little brat is starting to interfere with business — I'm having trouble concentrating on anything but her, and worse yet, I find myself excited by the fact.

I turn my attention back to my phone for a moment. There's a text on it from one of my men, alerting me about a potential informant he's found with a link to the police. Without a second thought, I text back the go-ahead to end the informant's life, and I know my wishes will be carried out in a matter of hours.

I've built a reputation in the Georgian mafia as a man whose demands are never taken lightly. I've earned every ounce of the respect I've garnered, through both careful politicking and old-fashioned fear. I've risen from the ashes of a war-torn childhood to become one of the most feared hitmen this side of the Atlantic, and I'm quickly establishing a branch-empire of my own out here, free to carry on my business however I choose. When I speak, men listen.

So why is this idle and unchallenged rich girl's charm able to sway me?

Putting my phone away, I step out the door onto a terrace that wraps around the side of the villa, leading to the hallway near the guest wing. As I do, I pass by a couple of my men on break, chatting idly over a couple of beers. I catch traces of their conversation — nothing but banter over the family back home, pretty ladies they've seen out in the city, and how they plan to spend the money from this haul. I give them a nod as I pass, and they respectfully rise as I walk by.

Those men are my comrades. We've all had each other's backs from the very beginning, helping and supporting one another as we carved out this strange living arrangement of ours. We grew up poor. Georgian-poor. And when we carry off these young girls for ransom, we do so knowing full well where we come from and where they came from. They're nothing like us. They pass their time and extravagant wealth with idle playthings like cars and clothes and luxurious trips, and they care for none of it.

That just makes me feel all the more furious over the feelings growing within me, about the undeniable care I've gotten for Delaney.

It feels strange to admit it to myself. If I feel this way about a girl born into a class so very far above my own, what does that make me? A class traitor? Am I turning against my own roots, against the poverty and war-torn land that forged me into the hitman I've become? Have I forgotten where I come from?

The questions that plague me as I pause to look out onto the sea before heading back inside only agitate me more. I feel like crawling outside my skin, a pent-up energy inside me desperate to get out. And the more my thoughts dwell near Delaney, the more desire I feel for her.

When I took her captive, I found a certain pleasure in being able to toy with someone who was so far above my station in upbringing — humbling the globe-trotting cheerleader and giving her a taste of subjugation. Now, though, so much more excites me about her. She's cleverer than she realizes or cares to realize. Even that infuriates me. Her natural talents would get a Georgian woman farther in life than most could ever aspire to, but Delaney has been content to squander it all on idle distractions.

But there's something in her beyond that. Something is making her realize that there's more to life than what she has. I wonder whether she's truly realizing from this time in captivity how much she could get out of life, and how much of it truly matters.

I roll my eyes at my own thoughts. I have neither time nor patience to hold this young woman's hand through self-discovery, but I could hold her hand through other things.

I find myself slowing down as I pass by her door, my eyes drifting to it for a moment. Part of me wants to go inside, chat with her, get to know her more like I did on the rooftop in the moonlight. My mind started to tell me things I should share, maybe to test whether there really is something to this girl I've developed annoying affections for.

But as I raise my hand to the door, a sound gives me pause, and I lean in, furrowing my brow. I can hear something moving against bedsheets, a rhythmic sound I'd recognize anywhere, and the stifled sounds of gasps. A smile comes across my face, and I feel my cock stiffening in my pants.

Without warning, I push the door open and step in to her surprised gasp.

Delaney withdraws her errant hand from between her thighs, pulling the sheets of her bed up to cover herself with a bright-red face as I step forward, my smile splitting into a grin as I close the door behind me.

"Darios!" she gasps, closing her legs despite her cherry-red face, "could you at least *knock*?!"

"Clearly I shouldn't," I say, taking in the sight of her. And what a sight it is. She's stripped her dress off, leaving herself in her underwear as she tries to 'entertain' herself in bed. "Especially when my girl is getting up to no good like this." I step closer to the bed, looming over her as she looks up at me.

"Well…" she stammers, biting her lip as she claws for an excuse, "it's not like I have anything else to pass the time with. You could have at least given me a Kindle to read on or something."

"Listen to you," I growl, crossing my thick arms. "You get bored, so you find such a *sinful* thing to kill time with," I say as I take her chin in my hands, but she pulls her head away, her face a defiant pout. "And when I walk in on you, you complain that I haven't gotten you enough trinkets to distract you with?"

"You almost make it sound like I'm staying here

voluntarily," she replies, an edge to her voice that I recognize as her testing me. The girl likes to play with fire. I can imagine what she was thinking of when she was touching herself. I'm wearing a white button-down that's partly unbuttoned for the heat and rolled up to my elbows. My pants are brown, and my stubble has grown past the point where I'd usually shave it.

"I wonder," I say, tilting my head to the side, "does your dad let you get away with this kind of misbehaving?"

"Hey!" she protests, but I take a step forward, putting a knee on the bed, and her eyes widen, making no move to stop me.

"Does he let you make these kinds of demands without any punishment? Does he just let you touch yourself whenever you like?" My voice is teasing, but her face is blushing furiously, her mouth falling open a little, at a loss for words in the haze that is her mind right now. She's already keyed up from what she was doing to herself. All I'm doing now is torturing her further.

"He never stops me from anything," Delaney says to my surprise, and I can hear the tinge of disappointment in her voice. A feeling I plan to amend.

"Well then, *chemo okro*," I say, unbuttoning my shirt after kicking my shoes off, "what makes you think I'll do the same?"

"I'm not running away," she says, her voice barely

more than a breath as she looks up at me, her reclining form taunting my every nerve, "so what are you going to do to stop me?"

I toss my shirt aside and reach down, my iron grip taking a hold of the front of her panties with both hands and ripping the fabric apart, to Delaney's gasp. "That was my only pair!" she yelps, looking up at me with wide eyes.

"If you're so set on finding dirty ways to have fun," I growl into her ear, feeling the shiver down her back, "then you won't be needing those, will you?"

She looks up at me, her body practically trembling with need and desire for me. Her hand starts to move up to my rippling abs, but I grasp her by the wrist as she does, pulling her close to me. "Do you really think I'd reward you for behaving so disrespectfully?"

"I-" she stammers, "I'm sorry, I-"

"You just thought you'd get everything you asked for sweetly, like the spoiled little daddy's girl you know you are," I finished for her, leaning forward, holding her hand close, so very close to the chest she wants to run her hands over so dearly. "But I think I'm tired of seeing you get what you want so easily, princess." I lean in, whispering into her ear. "You'll have to beg me for what you want."

Before she can reply, I slip my hand under the

small of her back and lift her up, spinning her around so that her back is to me.

"You can't make m-" she starts, but I cover those pretty lips with my hand, drawing her into my chest and grinning into her neck as I let my teeth tease along the sensitive skin, feeling her heart race.

"You spoiled little brat," I growl into her ear as she breathes through her nose, her eyes closed as I grip her thigh with my other hand, "you think just because you've been taunting me with that tight ass and ruby lips all this time that I'd give you anything you wanted?" I let out a quiet laugh, sliding my hand up to her hips, brushing over her wet lips only a moment before pulling her ass back to feel my stiff, needy cock. "The world's been your plaything your whole life, but I'm going to make you *mine.*"

My words are accented by a slap on her asscheek, a sharp sound that makes her whimper, my hand still over her mouth. "Now, *sykhaara,* what do you ask of me?"

I release her mouth, and she gasps before finding her voice. "I...take my bra off," she says weakly.

I slip my finger into her pussy, hooking it inward and making her gasp. "What do you say?"

"P-please," she begs, music to my ears, "I want to feel you all over me and inside me. Please, Darios," she manages, and I withdraw my finger, a low rumble in my chest as I draw my hand up her side in reward, and her back arches to meet it.

"Good girl," I whisper in a low husk as my fingers unhook her bra and let it fall to the floor.

My hands reach around and grope her breasts, and she lets out a sigh as I revel in the feel of her stiff nipples under my hands, taking in every inch of her sensitive flesh before bringing my fingers to the nipples themselves and rubbing them, watching Delaney's mouth open wide as the feeling shoots through her body.

"Most people have sensitive tits," I growl into her ear, "but it's even better for you, isn't it?" She doesn't respond, knowing I've found a weak spot so quickly, and my teeth go to her neck as my fingers torment her nipples, and she lets out a gasp. I'm not even touching her wet cunt as I stimulate her, moving my fingers back and forth, in circles, gently flicking the erect nipples of her small breasts, her whole body stiffening in desire for me.

I suck at the flesh of her neck, my teeth grazing her skin and making her try to squirm away from me, but I don't allow it. "Oh no, princess," I say, "you asked for this, and you're going to get it." She lets out a gasp as I attack her again, thumbs flicking her tits and toying with them between my thumb and forefinger.

She feels me start to laugh as I brush against her neck. "What? Don't laugh at me!" she whines.

"It's funny," I say, "you were so terrified of my threat of keeping you for myself..." I bring a hand to her shoulder and bend her over and she takes in a breath for what's about to come. "...but here you're already giving yourself to me."

My cock slips into her cunt from behind, and she lets out a yelp as I enter her, hard, her insides already soaking wet with desire. Hunger for me. "Ohhh, fuck!" she lets out, hanging her head as she tries to support herself on shaky arms. I answer her cry with another sharp slap on the ass that makes her tighten around my shaft, my crown grinding against her deepest insides.

"Such language," I scold her, gripping her hips with both hands as I pull her back onto me, practically holding her up as I start to buck into her. The scent of her pussy reaches me, spurring me on as I grind my cock against her inner walls, and she feels so wonderfully tight on me. She's made to rest around my cock, it would seem.

"Darios," she whimpers, "Darios, please don't stop!"

My shaft feels every inch of the insides of her slick walls as I pound into her, my swollen crown touching her innermost depths, and I let out a low moan as her honey floods me, the warmth sending a feeling of ecstasy through my whole body. I can't help it, I want this spoiled little brat. And I'm going to make her come for me.

My hands move around her hips, taking in the

feel of her flesh as I listen to the music of her little whimpers as I pound into her.

"I don't-" she gasps, "I don't want the guards to hear us!"

I take that as a challenge, and I smirk, starting to pound into her harder and faster, sticking my finger down to her clit and starting to rub it in a small circle around the swollen nub. She starts to gasp loudly but stops herself, gritting her teeth. "Please, Darios!"

"I'm holding up my end," I tease as she forces herself to look back at me, her face blushing at the sight of my broad body up to my balls inside her, looming over her from behind and drawing an imaginary zipper over my mouth. "You're the one who seems to have trouble keeping those pretty lips shut," I add with a meaningful buck deep into her cunt.

As I keep torturing her clit, I feel her start to tighten, already so close when I'd burst in on her, and she bends down to take a mouthful of sheets to stifle her voice, but I slap her on the ass again. "Head up, darling," I command, yanking her back and impaling her so far that she lets out a loud cry of ecstasy, her whole body tightening and relaxing as my cock is drowned in her fluids.

I feel waves of fire running from my massive crown up through my crotch, and her back arches as I slow in my bucking long enough to get a grip on her hips. As her orgasm starts to subside, her eyes flutter open, and she looks back at me with alarm. "What are you?"

I lean back, hoisting her up as she lets out a moan, carefully turning myself so that I'm sitting on the edge of the bed with her in my lap, my cock still stuffed into her swollen cunt. "How does it feel," I growl into her ear as I start bouncing her on my lap, making her head roll back helplessly as she moves up and down my shaft, "fucking your own captor, you hungry woman?" I grip her hips tight, and she can't respond, utterly overwhelmed by the angle of my cock as it grinds against her g-spot. Before long, I feel her body tightening again, and she lets out a soft gasp as she comes, and my machine-like rhythm doesn't stop, bouncing her on me like a toy as she feels more orgasms rack her body.

I can control every part of her from here, and I show off my power to her, twisting this way or that to change my angle, and each new position holds unspeakable ecstasy for her, her face red with passion as she breathes heavily. I can feel all of her so tight around me, and the way she desperately, greedily tries to scramble for control, to get more and more of my cock in her, tells me she's never felt so utterly whole. She rides my cock with surprising ability, hungry for more and seeming to have an unending appetite. I lose track of how many times I feel her come on me, but her exhaustion is nowhere in sight. I start to wonder just how starved for *real* pleasure this spoiled girl really is.

Just as she starts to get into the rhythm, though, I slow to a stop, and she looks back at me in confusion, instinctively giving me pouting eyes. "Don't think I'm letting you off that easily, girl," I taunt her, a cruel smile on my face.

"Please," she gasps, "please, let me...I want to..." her mind is a haze of ecstasy, and the sight of her struggling so amuses me. I raise a hand to her mouth and touch a finger to it, pushing my cock up into her to evoke another little gasp.

"Take your time, *sykhaara*," I coo, "you've been a good girl for me. Tell me what you want."

After a breath, she looks down at me, those endless eyes, sparkling blue as the Danube, heavy lids adorned by long blonde lashes. "Let me taste your cock," she lets spill out, her tone doing its best to hide the nervousness behind it. But I want to reassure her. I stroke her clit gently, and she closes her eyes and lets out a happy sigh before I slowly lift her off my cock as easily as if she were as light as a feather.

"All the sweeter with your honey, *chemo okro*," I say before placing her on the bed and leaning back, my spear sticking straight up and glistening with what she'd doused me in a few moments ago. Her eyes look at it as if it were a priceless treasure, and her hand reaches out, touching the rod and moving up and down it slowly, experimentally, her other hand touching my balls and rolling them around in her fingers.

In her small hands, my cock and balls seem all the more massive, more imposing. "How did all of that fit into me," she wonders out loud, eyes wide and wet as she twitches, a lingering wave of electricity from her orgasm shooting through her.

She looks up to me for approval, and I give a nod of my head. She crawls forward and brings those gorgeous lips to my crown, and it stiffens at their touch.

I lean my head back as she kisses the bulging crown, and the touch of her lips is warmer and more loving than I would have ever imagined. When I look back down at her, I meet her eyes as she breathes on my cock, and I see a little smile she's fighting to keep back as she opens her mouth, bringing it closer to my cock.

"You're enjoying this too much, you lusty little brat," I chide her, but as her mouth envelops my crown and she washes her tongue over it, I feel a fire in my chest as I look at her, feeling like I'm floating through the air on the ecstasy she brings me.

I've had women before, and I could have any woman I wanted, but none have made me feel like Delaney does. That fact is a spur in my side, even as I feel unprecedented pleasure as her tongue moves up and down the bottom of my shaft, massaging the sensitive cock and moaning as she savors the taste of it. The spoiled American girl has an effect on me...but my cock can return it just as powerfully.

I let her explore my cock, and again, her natural talent shines through, but there's no practiced method she's resorting to, no habitual motions she relies on to bring me the pleasure she's sending through me. Then something occurs to me, and I look at her with a new curiosity, running my hand through her golden locks as her eyes meet mine.

"You've never tasted cock before, have you, girl?"

She looks up, her eyes widening and she releases my crown hesitantly just long enough to pause and give her head a slight shake.

"I..." she starts, "You're the first person I've ever been with." She looks up at me again, nervousness in her eyes once more, and she looks terrified for a moment, desperately waiting for my approval. My face is unreadable. "I'm sorry, I should have-"

I cut her off as I reach forward, taking her chin in my hand. "Hush," I command. "If it didn't make a difference before, why should it now?"

I watch the fear in her eyes start to melt away, and when she goes back to my cock, it's with a renewed vigor that she takes as much of my shaft as she can fit into her mouth, and she lets out a sigh of absolute relief as she takes it in, nearly all of my cock vanishing into her hungry, needy mouth.

My muscles relax as I feel precum bead up at the

tip of my cock, and Delaney feels it too, bringing her mouth high up to the tip enough to taste it, moaning as she does, letting her lips linger on my cock.

"Do you like that, girl?" I ask, my voice a low husk.

"Mm-hm," she whimpers, too busy letting her tongue stroke my crown to nod.

"Then take more," I allow her, and I see her face redden and her breath pick up as she starts to attack my cock more passionately, more needily, more relentlessly as she traces the tip of her tongue around the rim of my crown, then down the bottom again, feeling every throb and twitch of my cock, and her fingers massage my balls as I feel them start to tighten.

My whole body tenses, and my jaw falls open and Delaney, ever the one to play with danger, opens her mouth wide to envelop the tip of my cock as she awaits what she's coaxed out of me so wantonly.

I let out a long, low groan as a shot of hot seed shoots up into her mouth, and she moans as she tastes it, using her tongue to torture my tip as she takes in shot after shot. I feel myself spilling out so much pearly seed, but she takes in all of it, swallowing what I give her like a reward she's been craving, and I look down at her as my cock twitches to see her hand at her clit again as I come inside her mouth.

When I'm finally spent, I nearly feel sore from

the force of my orgasm, and she licks my crown lovingly before drawing away from it, smiling up at me as I breathe deeply, the smell of our passion still in the air.

"Was I a good girl, Darios?" she asks, her voice sweet as honey as she crawls up to me, and I take her into my arms, letting her nestle into me with a satisfied sigh as I smile, our bodies glowing. My eyes watch her, narrowing for a moment, and I chuckle, stroking her hair as she curls into me, satisfied with my answer.

But as she gets comfortable, I look up at the ceiling. She feels so relaxed that she could fall asleep within a matter of moments. My heart, though, is in more turmoil than ever now that I realize I must come to grips with a question — no, a *fact* that is now more loud and clear than ever.

I took her virginity. I might be falling for this girl, but for her to give me something she'd held onto for so long...

I'm staring out the window at the sunrise, watching the sky split into gorgeous pink and golden hues as the Spanish countryside below is bathed in morning light. The trees are awash in pale illumination, the distant hills painted greenish gray at this early hour. I've been having trouble sleeping, which is not particularly surprising given the bizarreness of my surroundings, and so my body has been rousing like clockwork at the first rays of dawn.

At home, I slept with an expensive, opaque curtain hanging over my bay window so that the sunrise wouldn't wake me up before my alarm. But here, I don't even have a proper windowpane, much less a curtain to block out the light. Still, the air is clear and fresh, with just a trace of a balmy sea breeze from the Mediterranean pulsing just on the other side of the vast forest. Under normal circumstances, the scene would undoubtedly be Instagram-worthy, a location to feature on postcards home. Sometimes, when my mind wanders beyond the panic of my current predicament, I can zone myself out just enough to appreciate the beauty of the world outside my window.

But this morning, all I can think about is Darios.

The feeling of his hands coursing down my body, his fingertips grazing down every shivering inch of flesh with a possessive kind of greed. The sensation of his sensuous lips pressed against mine while he growls between kisses that I am his, that I belong to him. His fingers tangling in my long blonde hair and tugging me backward, forward, side to side like I'm merely a limp doll under his control. He handles my body like it's his most precious, practiced tool. Darios is powerful and menacing, a true force of nature — yet, in certain quiet moments I can almost feel a growing softness suspended between us. The fire in his eyes tames to a tender warmth rather than a raging inferno, and for a split second I wonder if maybe he could truly see something in me I haven't seen in years.

Like he might be looking deep inside me, reaching into my soul to withdraw a version of myself I haven't given breath to in ages. Like he sees the real me, buried under what feels like an eternity of make believe. How could it be that this hulking, untamed weapon of a man can strip me down so easily?

I swallow hard, my hands uncontrollably clutching at the ancient, wooden window sill as I stare out over the awakening land. I rest my forehead against the worn wall and close my eyes, only to realize that Darios's image is still fresh in my mind, that beautiful and cruel face gazing back at me even in the dark depths of my own thoughts.

I can't escape him even when I dream at night, fitfully tossing and turning in my stark white sheets still faintly stained with his seed. Last night I dreamed that we were tangled up together, wrapped in each other's arms as we made passionate love on the shores of the Mediterranean, the waves crashing playfully over us until the tide rose to wash us out to sea. As the water filled my lungs, I couldn't even break away from him to gasp for air. Our bodies, still enraptured in mutual pleasure, sank deeper and deeper under the surface until all light faded... and I woke up coughing, my forehead dewy with sweat.

Darios has infiltrated every nerve in my body and thought in my head.

I can't help but feel weakened, defeated. Like I've allowed a true predator to creep into my formerly guarded heart and seize control. He stalks through my mind and soul with those dark eyes trained on me all the time, keeping watch over me even when he's nowhere near. I find myself watching the door, anxiously awaiting his return. I can't eat. I can hardly sleep. Darios has settled into my bones like a powerful disease, bringing me to my knees.

But despite all these fears and pains I still feel giddy when I hear footsteps approaching. It's very rarely Darios, as there is a constant ebb and flow of surly guards tromping by, stopping in to bring me food and water or simply just to check in on me and make sure I'm still in my room. I have noticed a slight decrease in the frequency of these visits, however, and I assume that has something to do with the fact that I was attacked by one of the guards only a couple days ago. I don't know if Darios has ordered the guards to give me more space and privacy or if the guards are simply too put off by the sour fate of one of their own after crossing me. Either way, I do appreciate having a little more time to myself, even if I do spend the whole time wishing that Darios would come back.

I know that the morning guard will be coming in anytime now to bring me a bowl of lumpy porridge and perhaps a thin slice of melon. As of lately the porridge has been slightly less cold and colorless, as though Darios has been actively trying to make my stay here a bit less torturous. I still don't want to even touch the food with the occasional exception of the accompanying fruit or crusty bread, but it's a nice gesture all the same.

Almost like he's been summoned by my thoughts,

there's a curt knock at the door and I spin around to watch the morning guard come trudging in holding a tray of honeydew slices and a croissant. My eyes widen at the sight of a much more palatable breakfast than the usual fare, and then I realize that this is also a different guard than the one who has been checking in on me every morning. He doesn't look particularly interesting or even that different, with the exception of a long, mottled scar marring his jaw on the left side of his face.

"You're not my usual morning guard," I comment abruptly. He looks up at me, a little startled, like he hadn't realized I even possessed the ability to speak. "And the food is different, too," I add.

"Yes. Ambrosi has other matters to tend to this morning," the guard replies gruffly, setting the tray down on my bed as I approach slowly. I see a glint of something shiny poking out of his jacket pocket and for a moment I freeze up, thinking it's a gun or a knife. But then it hits me. It's not a weapon at all — it's a cell phone. And judging by the sparkly silver casing, it belongs to Caitlin. Suddenly, a rather risky idea comes to mind.

"Oh. Well, um, good morning. What's your name?" I ask, tilting my head to one side innocently.

The man glowers at me for a second and then grunts, "Eduard."

"That's a lovely name. I-I had a teacher back home with that name. He taught math. Are you good at math? I was never very good at it," I lie hastily. I'm actually pretty damn talented in mathematics, though you would never guess it from my lack of class participation or interest. Either way, I needed to keep him talking long enough to figure out how I might weasel that cell phone out of his pocket. I assume it might be dead by now, but if it's not… well, that's a risk I need to take.

"School was pointless," Eduard responds, shrugging. But I can tell he's starting to get a little interested in me. It's time to ramp up the charm.

I roll my eyes and groan sympathetically. "Oh, I know. I hated school. So glad I graduated so I don't have to learn about polynomials and vectors anymore. *So* boring, right?"

Eduard nods, crossing his arms over his chest. "I don't like learning."

"Who does? Ugh, it's not like any of that stuff even matters in the real world anyway," I agree excitedly, taking a few sultry steps closer. I bite my lip and glance up at him, widening my big blue eyes at him. He regards me a little dubiously at first, but when I get close enough, I just pick up the croissant and take a slow, dainty little bite out of it, making a big show of holding it in front of my mouth. I know it looks blatantly phallic, which is exactly my intention.

"Mmm. Oh my god, this is *so* good," I moan, licking my lips. Eduard is transfixed, and I know I've caught him in my trap. Just as predicted. Men are so easy. Well, most men anyway.

"It's from the bakery in the village," he says quietly, his eyes never leaving my lips as I chew. I nod, batting my eyelashes at him, trying to look genuinely interested.

"You're kidding? Oh, well it's amazing. So buttery. Almost melts in my mouth," I remark, tilting my head back slightly, as though in ecstasy. I'm not totally exaggerating, as this croissant actually is leagues better than anything else I've eaten in days. And Eduard is still just staring at me, open-mouthed, like he's never seen anything so delicious and fascinating in his life. I wonder how long it's been since he last had any intimate contact with a woman. No wonder this is so easy.

I step up to him and seductively set my hand on his chest, my fingers dainty and slender against his bulging pectoral muscles. He stares at my hand, but I need to distract him. So I raise the croissant to his lips and murmur, "You just *have* to take a bite. This is amazing."

His eyes are focused on my face as he takes a tentative bite, while my other hand delicately reaches into his pocket and slips the phone out. The poor oaf is so enraptured that he doesn't even notice. I feed him a couple more bites just to keep him distracted while I secretly drop the phone onto the bed right behind me. To cinch the deal, I then take a bite of the croissant as I sit down, the phone successfully hidden under my butt. I cross my legs and finish off the croissant in one bite, licking my fingertips while staring up at Eduard. He blinks dumbly down at me.

"I'm so glad to have met you today," I murmur, twirling a lock of my hair and smiling.

"M-Me, too," he replies, a little breathlessly. I can see the faint outline of his cock straining against the front of his trousers, already hard for me. But I need to shut this down fast, before anything else can transpire between us. I have what I need, and now he has to get out of here.

"Well, I guess you should go," I pout sadly. "The last guy who stayed in my room too long got thrown out that window, and I would hate for something like that to happen to you."

Eduard seems to snap back to reality. A look of genuine worry crosses his face and he nods, swiveling around and hurrying out of the room, giving me a final glance back over his shoulder as he closes the door behind him.

As soon as I hear his footsteps fading down the hallway I pull the phone into my hands and frantically turn it on, my heart pounding. The little battery symbol in the corner of the screen is red, with the power only at four percent. I open the dial keyboard and rack my brain for a number to call. The only number I have memorized is Brandon's.

In a frenzy, my shaking thumbs punch in his phone number and I listen to the rings, both anticipating and dreading the sound of his voice. I've done my best to forget about him and his stalker-like tendencies. Brandon is not someone I ever hoped to talk to again, and here I am calling him in my moment of crisis. I know he is going to lecture me, belittle me. Curse me for being so stupid. He's going to gloat that he was right, that he knew I would meet a terrible fate if I abandoned him for Europe. I don't want him to be right. And I really don't want to give him any power over me.

I never loved him, and I don't think he loved me — just the idea of owning and controlling me. He just wanted to be the one to deflower and ruin me. And not because he loved me and wanted to show me pleasure, but because he wanted the bragging rights. To be able to say he was the one who fucked the ice queen. He wants to place me up on a dusty shelf and keep me cooped up at home while he roamed the world freely. I shudder as I hear his familiar voice flooding into my ear.

"Hey, baby girl. Long-time no talk," Brandon says smugly.

In the next moment, several things happen all at once. The phone beeps twice and dies before I can even respond. The thought occurs to me that Brandon should not be expecting me on the other end of the line, since this is Caitlin's phone — and therefore, it only makes sense that he would be addressing Caitlin as baby girl.

He never even called *me* baby girl. What is going on? And for how long?

And then a flurry of deafening gunshots ring out, shattering my thoughts.

DARIOS

*J*run down the hallway as the sounds of bullets hitting the walls echoes around my head, and I can hear the girls' screaming in the distance. I run by the entrance to the terrace, only to see one of my men slumped dead against the edge, bullet holes in his chest. I curse and take cover behind the wall and pull out my phone, turning on the transceiver we use to communicate.

"Men! Remember your training and get into position, stick to procedure — this isn't a drill, we're under attack!"

"Who the fuck is shooting at us?" a voice comes back, the sound of gunfire in the background.

"Fucking mercenaries," growls another voice, and I feel fury swelling up in my heart. Could this be one of the parents taking justice into their own hands? This was something I'd thought about in the past, but my silencing tactics have proven effective up until now. I grip the pistol in my hand and crawl out onto the terrace, taking the bloody rifle from my dead man's hands and reloading it before heading back into the house and slinging it over my shoulder as I run.

One of my guards emerges from a room with a terrified Lyssa in his grasp, and both of them look to me as I approach, my man looking to me for direction.

"Get her to the cellar," I order in my native tongue, pointing down the hallway. "Take the old servants' staircase hidden in the laundry room to the right. Keep her head low and covered, they may not have men on the inside yet, but bullets still ricochet. You hear me?" I add looking the uneasy man in the eyes meaningfully.

Taking a breath and finding the confidence he'd forgotten, he nods resolutely. "Yes, sir!" Lyssa can't understand a word of Georgian, so she just looks to both of us with terror in her eyes, but I get her attention and point to her guard.

"He's going to get you to safety," I say in English, "if you leave his side, your life is in your own hands, understand, girl?"

"Y-yes!" she blurts, nodding and clinging to her guard, who nods to me and takes off, following my directions with his pistol out and his eyes alert.

I make my way around towards the dining hall —

I have to make rounds of the whole perimeter, but my thoughts are stuck on the safety of one person above all the rest.

"Do we have eyes on Delaney?" I bark over the phone, and there's a silence from the other men. "*Well?*"

"None here, sir," reports the guard assigned to her wing of the house, "she was in her room when the fighting started, and I took to the windows on the north wing to secure the-"

I curse, changing my direction and sprinting towards the guest wing, ignoring the rest of his statement. "Very well, I'm on it — why don't I hear fire from the rooftop? I want men with rifles in the tower *now*, we had those barricades installed up there for a reason."

"On it, sir," another couple of voices chime in near unison.

"Caitlin, what about her?" I shout.

"We were separated," her guard says back, sounding injured. "I had her near the entrance to the dining hall, but she bolted when a stray bullet caught me in the shoulder."

I swear. "What's your condition?"

"Don't mind me," he chuckles, "I've got more than enough muscle to take a few of these bastards' cheap bullets."

"Good man," I say, taking a short detour in my route. The dining hall is on the way to the guest wing, but if there were bullets flying into the room there, that means the attackers are trying to get in quickly, probably nearby.

I make my way down the hallway leading to the dining hall when the window about ten feet from me shatters, and my eyes widen at the sight of a grenade clattering to the ground. On pure instinct, my body responds by rushing towards it and kicking it back out the window, and I hear it go off before it even hits the ground, the sound of men shouting in pain is music to my ears as their own weapon blows up in their faces. I don't have much time.

I ready my rifle and appear at the window, looking at the three men down below recovering from the blast that killed what looks like two others. I take aim, and three quick shots later, there are five dead men on the ground below me.

Before their allies can return fire, I disappear from the window, rushing to the dining room door and kicking it open. I hear a shriek, and a butcher's knife comes flying at me from across the room. I only have a moment to react, moving to the side as it sinks into the wooden door behind me.

I raise my pistol to shoot the attacker, but upon seeing me, Caitlin throws her hands up with wide eyes, her face white as she crouches behind a barricade of kitchen tables she's erected for herself. "Oh my god I'm so sorry, I'm so sorry, oh my god, I didn't know it was you, please don't shoot!"

I swear under my breath as I rush forward, tossing the table barricade like a toy before grabbing her wrist and dragging her with me as I head for the opposite end of the dining room. "Where is your guard?"

With a shaking hand, Caitlin gestures to the opposite side of the room, where I see my man's body, having bled out from a new injury to the neck. Grunting, I just tug her along beside me, raising my phone.

"I need a man at the dining hall, now! Redirect other reinforcements to the foyer, I dealt with the incursion at this wing."

"Yes sir!" a few voices chime.

As we exit the room, my eyes focus on the window to my right in the next hallway out. There's a grappling hook lodged in it. I shove Caitlin behind me as I ready my pistol, and the moment a man's face appears, I fire, and Caitlin shrieks as he vanishes with a spattering of red on the windowsill.

A few moments later, one of my guards arrives, and I nod to him, gesturing to Caitlin. "Get her to the cellar with the rest, there's a passage down the hall to the left. She's shaken, but she can run, can't you?" I add to her, making sure she's responsive. It's not unusual for people new to combat to go unresponsive and into shock at the first sight of real violence — far more so for these sheltered American girls.

But she nods, swallows, and manages a "Yeah, yeah I can run!" as my guard comes to her side and holds her close to him. She instinctively wraps her hands around his arm, and he nods to me.

As they leave, I proceed to the guest wing, raising my phone again. "What's the status on the foyer?"

"We've repelled them, sir!" one of my lieutenants reports proudly, "But we're not out of hot water yet — they retreated and joined the men heading for the guest wing."

Fuck.

"Good," I say, "secure the other wings and ensure the girls headed for the cellar are well guarded — I don't want enemies coming within a fucking kilometer of that cellar, do you hear me?"

"Yes sir! What about the guest wing?"

"I'll handle that," I say, and while the pause on the other end tells me my men are worried about my safety, they know far better than to question me.

"Understood. Good luck, sir," my lieutenant says.

I tear down the hallway to the guest wing, but as I hear voices I don't recognize around the corner, I press my body up against the wall and listen.

"Did you find her?" a man says, and the voice makes my eyes widen. They're speaking in Georgian.

"Bitch must have gotten away when we stormed in," another says, and I hear his footsteps coming closer to me. My mind races. Why would there be Georgian mercenaries all the way out here? Why wouldn't the parents have hired Americans or even local Spaniards for the job? The conclusion is looking me in the face — these can't be just mercenaries. But why else would they be trying to take the girls away?

My thoughts are cut short as the footsteps tell me the man is right around the corner. Without another moment to spare, I move around the corner and reach around the man's neck before he can react. His eyes are still wide with surprise when I snap his neck and fire off two shots into the man standing behind him.

The two men drop, but my eyes are on Delaney's door — it's open. I sprint towards it, pistol out in one hand, and I draw my knife in the other, my rifle firmly around my shoulders.

I reach Delaney's room just as a man holding a raised pistol emerges, and I grab his wrist and twist it up just as he fires, sending dust raining over us as I slash his throat with my knife before he can scream. There are two men in the room behind him who both raise their guns, but I take cover on the other side of the doorframe as bullets fly out. I clench my jaw. Delaney isn't in her room, so I don't have time to tangle with these fools.

Remembering the grenade that I kicked out the window, I glance down at the dead mercenary's body and spot a glinting metal ball on his belt. I blind fire a few suppressing shots into the room as I reach for it, and I pull the pin out with my teeth before hurling the grenade into the room and pulling the wooden door shut.

I hear a man scream from inside as I turn to proceed down the hallway, and the door gets blasted off its hinges behind me as the two men inside are silenced.

I have my pistol raised as I round the next corner, but the silence there is deafening. Beyond it is a staircase that leads to the third floor, where my room is located. I didn't see Delaney on the way up here, so if she took off, then this is the only way she must have gone. I bound up the stairs, my heart pounding furiously.

I hear Delaney's terrified scream, and I quicken my pace, crouching down as I move to keep silent as I reach the top of the stairs. There's a corner that turns off to the north, leading to the door to my quarters, the master bedroom.

I hear heavy footsteps that don't belong to Delaney, and my muscles tense, ready to kill, but I hear a voice as Delaney rattles the door to my room, which is always locked.

"This isn't personal," the cruel, accented voice says in English. "If it were up to me, I'd just take you for myself. I bet a little cunt like you would be nice and tight around my cock all the way back to Georgia when this job is over. Shame we have to kill you all — our clients just don't appreciate fine pussy like I do."

I hear the cocking of a gun and Delaney's scream, and I whirl around the corner with my knife out.

The man who turns to look at me is a little farther than I thought, though, and he tries to bring his gun around to shoot me with a shouted curse. My knife slashes at his hand, making him drop the gun, which clatters to the ground, and I kick it to the wall before he can reach down.

His hand is bleeding profusely, but his eyes are bloodshot with fury, and he uses his other hand to draw a knife of his own as we square off. He lunges in, but I'm too quick for him, sidestepping him and coming in for a counterattack that he just barely parries with his wrist. He doesn't see my knee coming into his chest, though, and he nearly doubles over with a grunt as I knock the wind out of him.

My eyes catch a glimpse of Delaney cowering at the door, her eyes wide as she watches us fight. My enemy takes a blind hook aimed at my head, but I duck, and while his attention is distracted for a fraction of a second, I deliver a swift kick to his knee, making it crumple inwards with a sickening crack, and he howls in pain as he falls to the ground before I end his suffering, plunging my knife into his neck and watching the life drain from his eyes, his muscles giving out and his body going limp.

I rise up slowly, standing over his body as I turn to look at Delaney, who's breathing almost as heavily as I am. She doesn't stare for long, though, before standing up and rushing to me, and I catch her in my arms, lifting her up off her feet in a tight embrace as she sobs into my shoulder. When I set her down at last, I stroke her back, shushing her quietly as I reassure her.

"You're safe, Delaney, you're safe."

"I thought I was going to…" she starts, tears streaming down her face, but I take her by the hand, and kiss her tears away before looking her in the eyes.

"Let's not talk about that — come on, we'll be safer in my bedroom." She nods hurriedly, and I lead her to the door, unlocking it and closing it behind us before I rush to the window on the east side of the room, overlooking the entrance to the estate.

I pick up a pair of binoculars from my desk and use them to look over the grounds, and I smile at what I see. My men have routed the enemy — mercenaries are retreating in large numbers. There must have been nearly two-dozen of them when they came, judging by how many are in retreat. Then my gaze falls on one man in particular, and I feel my blood boiling, knuckles white on the binoculars.

"What do you see?" Delaney asks, cautiously stepping closer while keeping her distance from the window opening itself.

The red-haired man leading the retreat is unmistakable, and he casts a glance over his shoulder as he and his men vanish behind the cliffs, staring right up at my window ruefully. I can see his prosthetic hand clenched, his eyes full of hate.

"His name is Luka," I say, lowering my binoculars. "He and I have history."

"Is...is he some old accomplice?" Delaney ventures, biting her lip.

"Back in the war," I say grimly. "A lifetime ago, we fought side by side, but he sold my men and I out to the Russians. I hit him back a few years ago, though — hard. If he's here, then this attack might very well be some kind of power play on his part."

Delaney is about to speak, but my phone rings out with the sound of one of my lieutenant's voices.

"Sir! They're routed! We've done it!" I can hear the sounds of cheering in the background, and I smile. My men are talented, and it was their skill that complemented my command well.

"I can see that," I say, glancing out the window again. "Well done, all around. Are the girls secure?"

"We have two of them," he reports back, "did you find-"

"Delaney is with me," I say, putting my arm around her, and she smiles up at me, melting into my side, and I can feel how safe she feels around me. "For now, stay put and secure the perimeter, but do not pursue. I don't want us leaving this place exposed, and I don't want any heroes risking their lives in those cliffs — Luka is leading them."

"...are you sure, sir?" the voice asks, tinged with contempt for the man I named.

"Do I ever speak uncertainly?" I shoot back. "See that my orders are carried out. Now."

"Yes, sir!" the voice says, and I put my phone away as I look down to Delaney, putting both hands around her hips and squeezing them gently.

"Darios," she says in a quiet voice, her eyes steady on me, "I...I didn't think anyone would come for me. And I never thought I'd see someone do what you did, especially not for me."

"You're special, Delaney," I say, pulling her close to me, and she wraps her arms around my stomach, hugging into me for comfort. "I would never let anyone touch you — not one of my men, and certainly not my enemies." I pause for a moment, and I feel my instincts winning over my colder judgement in what I say next, but the adrenaline of the moment doesn't let me deny my heart any longer. "This is more than what I took you here for — this is a personal entanglement I never wanted any of you to get caught up in, especially not you," I add, cupping her face in my hands and kissing her forehead. "Delaney, if you wish, I will return you to your parents while I take care of this blood-feud. The other girls are already set to be ransomed soon, but your safety is the most important to me."

She looks up at me with shining eyes, and she bites her lip. For the briefest moment, I see a thoughtful look on her face, but the next moment, she hugs me tight, our hearts pounding against each other.

"I couldn't leave your side, Darios," she breathes, squeezing me. "I'm not going anywhere — I'm staying right here, with you."

I look at her, a smile on my hardened face as my hands slide down to her ass, squeezing it gently, then more firmly, pulling her hips against my hardening cock as I lean in to whisper into her ear, my voice a low husk.

"Then show me that you are mine."

 move towards the bed and toss her on it roughly, my adrenaline still pounding through my system as I hear her gasp when she hits the mattress.

My bed is huge and firm, with silken black sheets that I keep neatly made on the mattress. But I spend no time focusing on what's around me — not anymore. Right now, my body is spurring me forward to claim the woman before me, and nothing in the world could keep me from her.

I listen to her sigh as I pull her dress off, leaving her completely and utterly exposed before me, her chest rising and falling quickly as her own adrenaline makes her squirm on the bed sheets. My eyes ravish her as I rip my shirt off, hearing some of the fabric tear in my hurry to get it off my broad shoulders, muscles swollen from the strain I've put them through in the past few minutes.

Delaney's eyes are filled with desire as they look up at me, my body a statue for her to gaze at, looming over her. Those blue eyes of hers are endless, full of innocence despite everything that's happened in the past few days. I've pushed her to her breaking point, very possibly beyond, and still, she endures.

I smile, wondering if her body will prove to have as much endurance and hunger.

There's hesitation in her eyes, I realize. Those beautiful blue eyes are roving up and down my body, and I don't have to follow them to realize what she's noticing. I've gotten a number of scars on my body over the years, either from the combat I saw as a youth or injuries from my career with the mafia. There's one long knife wound scar on my side, a large scar from a bullet wound in my shoulder, and even some nearly-healed burn wounds on my hip from a motorcycle accident not too long ago.

"Tell me, girl," I say, striding over to the edge of the bed, my cock bulging in my pants as I flexed my hands and looked down at her hungrily. "You've never seen violence, have you?"

She swallows, licking her lips as she looks up at me cautiously, the thoughts of my scars dispelled from her by my gaze, at least for a moment. Finally, she shakes her head gently, her soft blonde tresses swaying as she does.

"Of course you haven't," I say, reaching down to her ankle and pulling her to the edge of the bed without warning, rubbing my thumb gently on her calf, "you've been in an ivory tower your whole life. Now, you're mine. How does it feel, girl?"

Before she can answer, I reach down, slipping my hand under her neck and pulling her up into a kiss, a deep, passionate kiss without tenderness or gentility. I want her, and I will have her. And as she moans softly into it, utterly taken off guard, she wraps her hands around my waist, wanting me just as badly.

She feels my sides, taking in every ripple and muscle, every inch of it a reminder that this body had been used to kill many people just a few moments ago — to kill for *her*. To protect her. And when her eyes rise to meet mine, I see them recognize me for the first time as a guardian, not just a killer.

"Dangerous," she finally answers, the word unsteady. I can tell she isn't sure how she feels about it — or rather, she isn't sure how to deal with the fact that her body seems to like it very, very much.

"Is that so?" I say, a smirk on my face as I slip my hands under her ass and pull her forward, hoisting her up into my arms. She instinctively puts her hands behind my neck for support, and she nods carefully as I turn and start to walk opposite the bed.

"I've never met someone who made me feel so...I'm not sure. Real?" she ventures, looking up at me with furrowed eyebrows. I chuckle, and her eyes turn to where I'm heading, then widen.

"You alone should be the one to listen to what your body wants," I say, stroking her back as I carry her to the window. "Because you're the only one who can *revel* in it as much as it deserves." As I reach the window with the gentle breeze blowing through it, I set her down on the open windowsill, holding her firmly on it, my hands a strong support for her.

Instinctively, she covers herself, glancing out the window with a little anxiety written on her face despite my strong grip. "Darios," she hisses, "I'm- I'm naked, someone could see!"

I grin, reaching behind her and unclasping her bra, pulling it away as she shivers. "At this height, that should be the least of your worries, *chemo kargo*."

Kneeling down, still holding onto her hips firmly as she grips the edges of the windowsill, I use my free hand to part her thighs and scoot her to the very edge of the windowsill. I hear her take a sharp breath as I lean forward, bringing my mouth to her exposed cunt. I can smell her lust on her, the rush of the moment still making her heart race and her face flush even as she glances over her shoulder.

In truth, this is more dangerous than I'd usually let things go. There were men with guns still retreating, and all it would take is for one of them to come back for a moment to see her, or one of my men to go after them and look over a shoulder to see Delaney's naked frame in the window, my hand the only thing keeping her up from a three-story fall. And I'm about to drive her to thrashing in ecstasy on that perch.

I let out a hungry groan as I bring my face to her cunt, and she sighs, squirming in my grip a little. "There are many sweet things about you, girl," I growl into her pussy, my voice low and full of desire, "but the taste of your cunt is one of the sweetest."

Before she can reply, I draw my tongue up her slit, and she shudders in pleasure, the heat of her cunt like an aura that only grows warmer as I draw my tongue up again, then again. Delaney is tense, though. I can feel her fear of the precipice she's on taking over, and she wants to struggle against her body's impulses, her desire for more pleasure, more ecstasy that only I can give her.

But I become relentless in my stroking, and once honey coats my mouth, I move up to her clit, bringing my tongue to a point and pressing up against the sensitive, swollen nub. As soon as it touches, she lets out a yelp that makes my hardened cock twitch in my pants.

My tongue starts lashing out relentlessly against her clit, and I hear Delaney's short, quick moans with each stroke, the tension within her wrestling with the pressure of desire building up, begging to be released.

Her back starts to lean backwards out the window despite herself, but my grip is secure, and my forearm muscles keep her steady on the edge as I torture her clit, tongue darting out in a machine-like rhythm as I drive her closer and closer to pleasure, not sparing her for a moment's respite as I let my tongue roll over her whole cunt, licking up the honey that spills out of her freely as I feel her start to tense.

"I tortured you last time," I say, "but now, I'll let you decide which is more cruel." Before she can ask what I mean, my tongue starts lashing out harder and faster than ever, digging deep into the swollen, needy folds of her cunt as my tongue absolutely torments Delaney's clit, her narrow hips trying to edge forward into me as I deal hard, quick strikes to that most sensitive spot.

"Oh my god, Darios," she sighs, a pained, tense squeak bursting with desire, with need for me. "Oh my god, I can't, I- I-" she struggles, and a grin tugs at the corners of my mouth as I don't let up, only growing more and more rhythmic and ever harder, the long strokes of my muscles not relenting with each contact unless I feel her tremble under me.

"*Ohhh, Darios!*" she cries out, heedless of the open window as I feel her muscles tighten, her thighs clenching around my head as her calves wrap around my neck, her whole body pressing up into me.

And even then, I don't stop.

My tongue keeps lashing out, even as she tries to pull back, her gasps growing desperate, and I turn my eyes up to her to see her cheeks flushed red, her jaw hanging agape as she fights to keep control over her body and the paralyzing sensations I'm over-whelming her every muscle with. Yet even as she struggles, she pushes into me further, hungering for more, *needing* more.

She's greedy. She's always been greedy, even for punishment, and now it's given her body an itch that only I can scratch. I let my tongue delve deep into her, flexing and filling up so much of her, then slowly pulling out and up to her clit as my strong hands hold her in place, one keeping her from death, the other keeping her thighs pried apart. Orgasm after orgasm rolls through her, racking her whole body as she grips the sides of the windowsill, letting out cries of bliss as her lower abdomen tightens and relaxes, pulsing and twitching with abandon, my hand the only thing keeping her from flailing out the window.

"I don't...I don't know how much more I can take," she whimpers, and my cock is threatening to burst from my pants, it's so thick.

I raise my head, taking her neck in my free hand and pulling her into a kiss, letting her taste her own honey with a low growl from my chest. "This is your punishment, brat," I growl as I undo my pants, letting my monstrously hard cock spring free.

"For what?" she breathes, opening those desperate blue eyes, licking her come from her lips.

"For making it impossible to get you out of my mind," I reply, and before she can answer, I fill her up with my cock.

Immediately, I feel her tighten around me, and she lets out a deep, satisfied sigh, melting into my hands as I hold her up. Any other woman would be a ragdoll by now as I start to buck into her, my own energy charging me with vigor, balls slapping against her ass as I deliver thrust after thrust, but Delaney is special.

"How much lust do you have, girl," I whisper, "that you can stay hungry for more after I've given you so much?"

"You drive me fucking crazy," she pouts, burying her face in my chest as I grip her hips, and I feel my cock arch upwards with tension, and she yelps as my bulging crown hits her g-spot. "Please, just don't stop!"

I take a fistful of her hair, tilting her head back and out the window as I lean over her while another orgasm shakes her whole body. "I like to hear you beg," I whisper into her ear, and I push myself into her to the hilt, her tight cunt desperately trying to get all of me as I overwhelm her, bucking her harder and faster, her breaths short as her eyes roll into the back of her head.

No woman has ever made my cock swell so much, dig so deep, seek so much in a woman's folds as Delaney. I took this spoiled woman like a prize, but now the unthinkable has happened, I realize.

I'm falling in love with her.

My bucking grows faster, my hips like a piston ramming in and out of her, but my cock feels so fucking natural in her pampered body that it fuels my anger that her beauty has transformed into pure, energetic passion.

"I need you, Darios," she whines, and my cock responds. I feel myself tightening within her, but I restrain myself for just a little while longer yet. I want to push Delaney to her limits.

She leans back, my cock bucking so far up into her that she's nearly being pushed off the ledge. Then I feel her tension building up with something stronger than she's experienced before, and her suddenly widening eyes tell me she feels it too.

I let my restraints loose, feeling my bulge swell fuller than ever inside her as I let out a groan, filling every inch of her cunt as she lets go of the windowsill reaching forward and wrapping her arms around my neck, totally relying on me to keep her up as I plough into her, feeling our tensions build up together to very high.

Finally, I let out a long, low groan as I feel myself

release within her just as what feels like a lifetime of tension unwinds within her, our voices mingled in satisfaction as shots of my seed spill out into her, filling her up as I slide back and forth, massaging both of us down from our orgasms. My cock twitches, releasing more and more of myself into her, and she bites her lip as though my cock is red-hot within her, clenching herself tight as I grind inside her, drawing her close to me and putting my forehead to hers.

"Fuck, Darios," she whispers, nearly limp in my grasp.

I chuckle, finally sliding myself out of her and picking her up, carrying her to my bed and laying her down, a pool of relieved woman and seed. "You keep surprising me, little girl," I say, massaging my cock and feeling her honey still on me. She smiles, curling her head into her shoulder bashfully before I give her hand a squeeze. "Come on, let's shower off. You should get acquainted with your new living quarters."

A few moments later, hot water is washing over both our bodies in my spacious shower, steam rising as the remains of my fight and our fucking get washed off my body.

Delaney's eyes are all over me, even more than mine are on her. Even after so many orgasms, I can see the arousal in her eyes as she looks at me. "Do I have a bullet hole in me," I ask, "or is it true what they say about you lustful American girls?"

She blushes and sticks her lip out at me, but there's a smirk under it. "When things get hot and heavy," she says, reaching out and stroking my half-mast cock gently, "I...get a little swept up in the action and don't get to appreciate all this at once," she says, gesturing to my whole, muscular body.

I gently turn Delaney around, lathering a little soap and running my hands over her whole body, exploring every inch of her as I kiss her soaking-wet neck. "What, you don't think that makes your captor all the more mysterious?" I tease, and she smiles, but even as she presses her ass into my cock, I can feel some hesitation in her.

"God, this is so messed up," she says, turning away a moment, "you really *are* my captor. It's easy to forget in all this rush, but..." She brings her hand across one of my scars gently, thoughtfully. "Those scars. Those are from..."

"From fights, Delaney," I say into her ear, a low growl. "Fights where men died. Some where I defended my life, some where I defended my comrades, and some where I was out to kill someone for one reason or another. This is my business, Delaney."

She shivers, and I turn her around, pressing her against the cool glass wall of the shower, a hand on either side of her as I look at her, water running from my wet, dark hair down my stubble-ridden face as my dark eyes pierce hers. I smile.

"I'm a killer, Delaney. I trade lives for pay, whether it's in ransom or blood money. You saw me kill today, and you might see me kill again." I lean forward and press my lips to hers, listening to her breath drawing in sharply. When I break the kiss, whisper into her ear, "And I don't plan to change that any time soon."

I turn over in bed and blink at the hulking mass of muscles lying beside me, my eyes drinking in every hard line and sharp curve with a sense of awe and disbelief. I still can't quite wrap my mind around what I've gotten myself into. My body aches in a dull, satisfying kind of way after being so forcefully manhandled by Darios. I can still feel the hard imprints of his hands on my skin, like he's tattooed me with his touch. Branded me forever more.

He's lying on his back with his chest calmly rising and falling ever so slightly, his dark eyes closed and a peaceful, unreadable expression on his handsome face. I have the strangest nervousness twisting in my gut, as though I've suddenly found myself lying naked in a cage next to a sleeping lion. At any moment, the predator could open up his fierce golden eyes and devour me in one unapologetic gulp.

But despite the residual — and healthy — fear I feel when I think about him, I can't deny that my survival instincts are quickly being overthrown by my desire for closeness. And not just with anyone; with Darios in particular. Because if I were truly desperate, it would make much more sense for me to pine after Brandon or literally anyone else from back home. Boys who are simple and harmless. Men who don't frighten me. I should long for some tall, foolish all-American footballer who just wants to hold my hand and ask me to prom. If I were smart, perhaps I would feel a small iota of longing for the kind of guy who doesn't scare me, but might just bore me to tears.

Instead, I am curled up next to a man who has committed terrible crimes. Darios is a kidnapper, a con man… a *murderer*. He should terrify me to my core and send me running in the opposite direction, but here I am. I bite my lip, fighting the urge to reach out and touch him, to test if he's really real or not. Sometimes in these quiet moments, I could almost imagine that this is all a big fever dream. A nightmare mashed up with the steamiest sex dream I've ever had. But the authentic ache in my muscles and the taste of him on my tongue reminds me that this is *real*. This is happening.

What would my parents think of me now? I can

just picture my mom's jaw dropping and her big blue eyes going wide with shock. She might even put down her beloved cell phone for once in her life and pay attention to me, even if it was just to scream at me in disgust. And my dad… god, he would fall to pieces if he saw me shacking up in some rundown Spanish villa with a Georgian serial murderer and his crew of likeminded bandits. Hell, he would lose his mind just at the prospect of his precious, virginal little girl in bed with *any* man, much less someone like Darios.

But a lot has changed since I hopped on that plane to Barcelona with my friends. I'm no longer the same apathetic, superficial pseudo-southern belle I was then. Without access to my phone, my money, my social media accounts, all the tenets that supported my reign of power as an alpha popular girl in high school, I have had to come to terms with who I really am underneath all of that.

I'm still not entirely sure how I feel about the girl behind the mask. And I'm not one hundred percent sure the mask is totally off just yet. I may be walking a new walk and talking a new talk but deep down, I still feel like I'm hiding myself. I suppose that's only natural, considering the fact that anyone should keep their guard up in such a sticky situation. I mean, I am literally surrounded by murderous men in the middle of a foreign country. I'm pretty much lying in a pit of snakes right now, and if I make one wrong move, I will undoubtedly get bitten. But Darios has certainly done his part to make me feel just a little bit safer. Having him on my side is one way to keep the other guys off my back. After what happened to the guard who tried to assault me, every other guy seems to give me a fairly wide berth. None of them want to meet the same dark fate.

I shiver to myself, closing my eyes to block out the memory of the guard falling through the open window, the sick crunch of his massive body hitting the ground below. It's still difficult to come to terms with the fact that Darios, the man whose arms encircle me and ravish me, is also a cold-blooded killer.

But then, I suppose, at least I can comfort myself with the fact that he killed for *me*.

Darios is resting so calmly that I can almost kid myself into ignoring his darker side. When he's asleep beside me he could almost be just any regular handsome man, exhausted after hours of passionate lovemaking. But the battle scars marking the length of his body help to shatter this illusion. He didn't get these scars from playing football or roughhousing with the boys. His body is a road map of every dark destination he's visited, every drop of blood he's spilled, every life he has brutally, expertly extinguished.

I swallow back a lump in my throat and survey the elegant, yet masculine cut of his strong jaw, peppered with dark stubble. My eyes follow upward to his ruddy cheeks and thick black brows, his gently hooked nose and sensual, full lips. His black hair is grown out quite a bit longer than the typical wholesome frat boy hair I'm used to seeing back in Savannah. I've grown up around neat military crops and trimmed-down crew cuts, men with smooth faces and easy, disarming smiles. Every attractive guy I knew growing up was essentially the same prototype with only a few miniscule discrepancies to set each separate model apart.

But Darios is different in every conceivable way. Nothing about him is dull or expected. He surprises me at every turn, and for once I don't have the upper hand. He knows just how to control me, how to mold me into whatever shape he wants — and I let him, because every time he touches me I am reduced to a puddle of obedient desire. Despite the innocent, wilting flower I put on around boys, I have never actually considered myself a very submissive or passive person. In fact, I usually like to be the one holding the reins. It's safer that way. Easier.

And now look at me. I'm putty in this man's hands. He has captivated me and intoxicated me, and in such a short time I have become painfully addicted to his attentions. I crave his touch and thirst for his voice. I dream of him when I sleep and I daydream about him when I'm awake. When he's thrusting inside of me, splitting me in two, I feel whole for the first time in my life. Like I've spent all my eighteen years just waiting for someone like Darios to burst in and change my life. Like I've been walking this earth in a sort of dazed dream all this time. And now I've stepped through a door into another world, a different reality in which I am no longer the same version of myself.

The Delaney Underwood who inhabits my body now is not the one who came to Europe some time ago. I've changed, and I owe it all to Darios. For better or for worse.

But part of me longs for some feeling of familiarity, some connection to my past. Sometimes I feel like I'm fumbling for footholds that I can't find, treading water endlessly in search of the shore. I know what I need. I have to talk to my friends. I need to remind myself that there's another world out there, outside this sinful bed I share with Darios.

And I need him to let me see them.

So I gingerly reach out and lay my hand on his chest, whispering, "Darios."

His eyes open slowly and he turns to look at me, immediately making my heart beat faster.

"Yes," he murmurs, covering my hand with one of his.

"I have something to ask you," I continue nervously. "I-I am worried about my friends. I just want to see them and make sure they're okay. Please."

Darios narrows his eyes at me suspiciously for a moment and I worry that he will be angry, but then he simply nods. "Of course. You have agreed to stay with me, and I will hold you to that vow. Your friends are in the basement panic room. Tomorrow morning, Lyssa will be ransomed back to her parents, but tonight you may stay with them if you like."

I sit up and lean over to kiss him on the cheek gratefully. "Thank you," I mumble.

"The guards should give you leave to do so. If they give you any trouble, call for me and I will… set them straight," Darios assures me.

I crawl out of his bed and pull on the oversized men's button-down shirt he's lending me, then give him one more appreciative smile before I head out down the stairs. Brushing my hair back behind my ears as I descend to the basement, I nod curtly at the two guards stationed near the entryway. To my pleasant surprise, they both stand aside for me to come through without a word. Being Darios's little mistress — or whatever I am — certainly has its perks.

"Darios has given me permission to see my friends," I tell the guard at the door. He unlocks the door and opens it to let me in. I step through into the dimly lit, dank little cellar and immediately Lyssa and Caitlin come running to me, throwing their arms around me.

"You're okay!" Lyssa exclaims.

"We were so worried," Caitlin cries, hugging me tightly.

"I'm fine," I reassure them, feeling an overwhelming surge of fondness for my friends. Seeing their familiar, albeit pale and horrified, faces is such a comfort. Neither of them look very good, which is to be expected considering our situation, but at least they're alive.

"Where have you been? I overheard one of the guards mention a while back that Megan went home with her family, but I didn't know what happened to you," Caitlin says, fidgeting anxiously.

"I was hoping maybe you got to go home, too," Lyssa adds with a shrug.

I sigh sadly. "No, I've been here the whole time. Have they been keeping you in the same place together all along?"

The girls shake their heads. "Nope. For a long time we were in separate rooms. It was so lonely and scary... I thought I was going crazy," Lyssa remarks with a visible shudder. Suddenly, I am reminded of the guy who attempted to sexually assault me and my blood runs cold.

"Wait — has anyone tried to hurt you? Either of you? There was one man who tried to hurt me but Darios, he saved me. If anyone has laid a finger on you, I will make them pay," I burst out. Lyssa hugs me again.

"No, no. I've just been quiet and keeping to myself. Nobody gave me any trouble," she says.

Caitlin looks a little troubled, though. "Well, there was one guy who tried to… touch me. But I spat in his face and he left me alone."

My mouth falls open and I take her hand instinctively. "Caitlin! You could've gotten killed! These guys — they're dangerous. They won't bat an eye at the thought of hurting you."

She shrugs. "For a while there I didn't care what happened to me. I was — I was so depressed I almost wanted one of them to hurt me. Just to have something happen. But ever since that big fight, I've been down here with Lyssa. I feel a lot better now that I'm not all alone up there."

My heart sinks. "Well, I have both good news and bad news," I begin, biting my lip. The girls both look at me expectantly. I go on. "Lyssa, you're going home tomorrow. Your mom has the ransom money. But Caitlin… that means you're going to be alone again."

I can see both happiness and pain etched in both of their pretty faces. Caitlin turns to Lyssa and hugs her, saying, "I don't care. I'm just happy you get to go home. Besides, I won't be alone now that you're here." She looks at me hopefully.

I don't have the heart to tell her that Darios probably won't let me stay with her the whole time, but I can't break her spirits any further. Not right now. "You're right. I will stay with you as much as I can.

This is a good thing, girls. Lyssa is going home! And can I just say, I am so, so happy to see you guys again. I missed you more than you know."

And it's true. I have longed for the companionship of my friends for so long, and now that we are reunited, however briefly, I want to make the most of it. So the three of us flop down on the pile of moth-eaten cushions on the floor and start catching up. We talk about our time here, Caitlin and Lyssa explaining how lonely they've been, how scared, and even how bored. After some prodding, I reluctantly tell them about my growing involvement with Darios. I explain how he saved my life, how I finally gave up my virginity to him.

I tell them about how I'm starting to fall for him, and they share their concerns at first, but once I explain more about my dynamic with him and everything he's done for me, they come around. But I notice Caitlin being cagey and quiet, which is very out of character for the girl who always has something to say.

"Hey, Cait. What's going on?" I ask, and she gives me a dodgy, teary-eyed look.

"Yeah, what's up, honey?" Lyssa adds, patting her arm sweetly.

Caitlin stares at the floor for several seconds, as though trying to build up the courage to say what's on her mind. Then she suddenly looks up and says,

"Delaney, I-I have to admit something. It's awful. And I will totally understand if you hate me—"

"What is it?" I interrupt, confused.

She rolls her eyes up to the ceiling and takes a long, deep breath before going on. She looks me right in the eyes and confesses tearfully, "I can't stand it anymore. I hate keeping secrets from you. You're my best friend and you need to know. I… I slept with Brandon."

There's a thick, heavy silence. Lyssa looks back and forth between us in horror, as though she's expecting me to fall back into my former ice queen persona and slap Caitlin across the face. I have to admit that there was a time I would have done exactly that. The old Delaney would have made it her sole mission to punish Caitlin for such an awful betrayal. My heart hammers in my chest for a moment as it dawns on me that I now understand why Brandon answered my call to him on her phone in that strange manner. They were sleeping together behind my back. The whole time he was pestering me to sleep with him, threatening to find some other girl to sleep with if I wouldn't, he was already cheating on me with my best friend.

But despite this betrayal, I can't even find the energy to be angry. I'm a little hurt, of course, but I'm realizing that as bizarre as it is, I am actually a little relieved. I have a perfectly good reason to ignore him, to cut him out of my life as I have wanted to do for so long. I am absolved of guilt.

"Please, please forgive me," Caitlin begs, clasping her hands together as a tear rolls down her cheek. I can't remember the last time I saw her cry. She's a tough girl. So it's all the more moving that she is so broken up about this.

"Cait, I honestly can't even be upset. I never loved him anyway. And yeah, this does hurt a little bit because you're my best friend. But in the end, he's just some stupid boy. I never want something like this to come between us. If I've learned anything from this whole crazy predicament we're stuck in, it's that I have way bigger things to worry about than guys like Brandon. He's not important. But our friendship… now, that is important," I tell her.

"I'm so sorry, Laney. It was so stupid, he came to me because he wanted to make you jealous and I just did it because I was jealous. You know, I was the most popular girl in school until you came along and I guess there was always a part of me that resented that. I was bitter. I was such an idiot. I can't believe I would be so stupid," Caitlin sobs.

"It's okay. We've all done things to hurt each other in the past. Petty, stupid things that don't matter anymore. We're better than this," I assure her, leaning over to hug her close. Lyssa joins in, wrapping her arms around us.

"I love you guys, and I swear we're gonna make it

out of this alive. And I promise that once we do, things will be different. I don't want to ever feel like I have to compete with my best friends. Nothing but love from here on out, okay?" I remark.

"Agreed," Caitlin mumbles, wiping her eyes.

"I love y'all so much," Lyssa says genuinely.

We spend the next few hours chatting about the old days, even laughing about the stupid things we did and the superficial lives we led back home. It's crazy to think about how much has changed in such a short amount of time. Halfway through the night, a guard comes to tell me that it's time to go, but I shake my head.

"No. You know what? I've been separated from my friends long enough. I'm going to stay here with them tonight. Darios told me not to let anyone stand in my way. I-I have free reign of the villa," I tell him firmly. Caitlin grabs at my hand anxiously, squeezing it as though trying to warn me to be more careful about how I talk to him. But I won't let this guy see my fear.

The guard stares at me for a long moment, sizing me up. I can tell he is not accustomed to girls talking back to him. But my mention of Darios seems to seal the deal, since he finally gives me a nod and replies, "Very well, then."

He closes the door, leaving me to pile onto the mishmash of pillows with my friends for the night, all three of us exhausted. We whisper amongst ourselves like we're fourteen years old and cuddled up at a sleepover together, just like old times, until finally we all drift off to sleep.

However, I am jostled awake an hour or so later by the sound of someone turning the door handle and pushing inside. I sit up, blinking in the darkness, trying to determine who the hell could be coming into the cellar at this hour. Something puts me on edge, my heart racing in my chest.

"Who is it? Who are you?" I hiss through the pitch black silence.

Heavy footsteps plod into the room and I seize up, anxiously awaiting the reply.

I stand up cautiously, squinting in the direction of the door. By now my two friends, both of whom are fairly heavy sleepers, are waking up. Lyssa mumbles sleepily, "What is it?"

"What are you doing?" Caitlin yawns.

"Someone is coming in," I say softly. "Stay back."

As the door opens further, there's just enough grayish light filtering through to cast the intruder in a wide, hulking silhouette. For a moment I dare to hope that it's just Darios coming to collect me and bring me to bed, but when the figure speaks, my heart sinks.

"The two of you go back to sleep. I have come under direct orders to retrieve Caitlin Thomas from the cellar. It's time to go," he says gruffly, with a heavy accent. It definitely isn't Darios, and something about him puts me on edge. I don't trust that he's working for Darios.

"Wait, what?" Caitlin says, standing up next to me and linking her arm with mine.

"You heard me," the man responds, taking several steps forward. I push Caitlin back behind me and Lyssa gets up to help me guard her from this strange man.

"No one is taking my friend anywhere without an explanation," I declare, fear and fury roiling inside of me. I'm terrified that this man is here to hurt us, to attack Caitlin the way that guard assaulted me. But this time, Darios is nowhere to be found, so who will save us?

"I do not have to explain myself to spoiled little American girls like you. This matter does not concern you. Back off. I will resort to brute force if necessary, *dzukna*," he snarls.

Lyssa retreats, clearly taking the guy at his word. But I plant my feet more firmly and shake my head, holding my arms outstretched. "No. Tell me what's going on. If you lay a finger on me, you'll have Darios to reckon with, and I don't think you want that," I counter sharply.

The man stops short, glowering down at me. My eyes have adjusted as best they can to the low light and I can now make out the craggy face of a slightly older man. I can see the outline of a crooked nose and beady black eyes. He's as intimidating physically as he is verbally, and I have to fight the urge to shrink away into the shadows.

"You are insolent. I pray that someday you are put back in your place," he says darkly. "If you must know, I am here to take Miss Thomas back to her family."

"What?" gasps Caitlin, emerging from behind me. "B-But my dad... he lost his job. My parents are almost broke. Th-they don't have the kind of money to buy me back."

"Oh my god, Cait," Lyssa breaks in, confused, but she'd just confirmed my suspicions. More than that, it explained so much, like why she so easily fell into bed with Brandon. She's been struggling with a huge secret, and it's made her act out in uncharacteristic ways. It breaks my heart to think that she didn't feel comfortable sharing her troubles with us. We shouldn't have to hide things from each other. I make a silent vow to be a better friend from now on.

"Why didn't you say anything?" I ask, giving my friend a worried look.

She shrugs and sighs. "I guess I was too embarrassed. You all have so much money and everything you want and I did, too, until... well, about six months ago my dad got laid off. The business is going under and we're not doing so well."

"I'm so sorry, Cait," I tell her genuinely. I can tell it wounds her deeply to admit weakness. She and I have always had that in common. Neither of us like for anyone to see us hurting. We always want to come off as strong and confident.

"Yeah, you should've told us. We would have helped you," Lyssa remarks. "What else are friends for?"

"None of this is important. Either way, they have the money. Come along," interrupts the man.

"I-I'm really going home?" Caitlin asks breathlessly. "This isn't a trick?"

The man nods. "It is time for you to go. Come with me."

"Wait, wait, wait. In the middle of the night? Since when is that how it works?" I pipe up, suspicious of this whole ordeal. Caitlin is more than willing to go along with this, and I definitely understand why, but I learned long ago that wishful thinking can end in bitter disappointment. Usually if something seems too good to be true, it probably is.

The man fixes me with a blistering glare. "You know nothing about how this works. Don't kid yourself. You think just because Darios has made you his little fuck-pet you suddenly have some kind of power? Don't be such a fool. You mean nothing to him and you are nothing to me. Now step aside."

"Laney, let the man do his job," Caitlin hisses in my ear. I can feel her positively bristling with excitement at the prospect of finally going home to her family.

"I just think we're being a little too eager about

this," I reply, taking her by the arm and trying to hold her back a little longer. "Where did your parents get the money? Why are you leaving right now instead of in the morning, like Lyssa? It just doesn't make sense..."

"Stop talking. That is enough," growls the man. He rushes forward and roughly grabs Caitlin's other arm, wrenching her away from me. "Maybe Darios enjoys indulging your impudence, but I do not. We are leaving. Now."

He starts dragging Caitlin away, and she turns to give us a reassuring smile, trying to put on a brave face. "Don't worry, y'all. I'll be okay. Lyssa, you're going home tomorrow. Delaney — thank you for looking out for us."

"Hurry up," barks her captor.

But a look of realization comes over her face and she says quickly, "Oh, uh, wait. I need to get something from my friend really fast. Then I'll come with you, okay? I won't fight you at all. I'm really excited to go, I swear."

The man heaves a frustrated sigh and releases her for a moment. She hurries over to me and says loudly, "Oh, thank you for holding onto my earring all this time, Delaney. I-I need to get it back so I can sell it when I get home. My parents are super broke right now, you know. So, I'll just, um, lean in and take it off—"

I'm confused at first, having forgotten that I'm

even wearing earrings, much less earrings that belong to Caitlin. But then she leans in close and whispers in a barely audible tone, "Do you want me to fill Brandon in on what's going on? I-I can talk to him when I get home."

I shake my head ever so slightly and she looks surprised for a split second, then recovers herself before the man can take notice of anything amiss. She takes off my earrings and tucks them into the pocket of her dress, giving me a wide smile, even though I can still see the confusion in her eyes. I can't explain it to her right now, but the truth is that I don't want Brandon to know what's happening to me. In fact, I don't want him to know anything about me at all anymore. I'm done with him, utterly and completely. I would rather die here than have to go crawling back to him.

"Well, thank you. I guess I'll, uh, see you guys later. Hang in there," Caitlin says, giving us a little wave as she walks back over to the door. Lyssa and I wave back at her and watch as the man guides her out, shutting the door behind him, leaving us alone in the stark blackness.

Lyssa and I do the only thing we can do and go back to our little sleep station. After I do my best to reassure her that all will be okay, she finally falls asleep and I sit there totally awake, thinking about what I should do. I have this burning voice in the back of my mind telling me this isn't right.

When morning comes, I have made up my mind. I gently awaken Lyssa and give her a tight hug and a goodbye, wishing her good luck. I promise that we'll see each other again soon, even though I don't know if that's a promise I can keep. And then I get up and go upstairs to confront Darios.

pull up at the compound after a long night of check-ins with past 'clients,' and I want to punch through a wall in frustration. Every family I visited, every person whose arm I twisted for information, none of them produced any leads. All of my past victims have been tight-lipped, thankfully, but I only ever get the same response from those who've been contacted by someone: they reached out to them asking probing questions, but nobody has a source. All anonymous calls. The callers could be anyone, and I'm left keeping my guard up in the dark.

This isn't an enemy I can just face head-on or blackmail. My suspicion is that Luka is greasing some palms in the media to get this stirred up against me while he rebuilds his old gang. Tracking him down is also a high priority, but I can't let myself become exposed in the process, so ensuring the silence of all past witnesses takes chief importance.

I walk across the villa grounds, feeling the morning dew on my face as I make my way towards the doors. Despite all the unease, I find myself happy to have such a place to come back to in the early hours of the morning. There is a certain antique stasis to the villa that serves as a rock for my psyche, as well as that of the ransomed girls.

Not that I try to comfort the brats, but it keeps them from panicking and becoming too much to manage.

And when things are amiss in this unchanging place, I can tell instantly. That's the sensation I get the moment I walk through the doors and start climbing the stairs to my room. The men nod to me as usual, but I can feel an uneasiness in the air that I can't quite place. I move past the men without much regard, though. I don't have time for pleasantries.

Up in my room, I take off my jacket and set my weapons aside, stepping over to a map of the city I have up on the wall as I cross my arms. My body wants to sleep, but I can't allow myself to rest, not while there are so many questions unanswered.

I have a few areas of the city circled, thumbtacks pushed into sites I know to be strongholds of local crime lords. If Luka is trying to build up enough support to take me down, then he'll have to be collaborating with one or more of them. I've already begun contemplating who will have to die first — the world will not miss such scum.

My name carries weight in Barcelona. I know the Spaniards resent me, but they must fear me if they are to be allowed to live. Each and every one of them, even the proudest, know that I am a threat. That's kept them in line for years, leaving me to carry on my trade unimpeded, but if Luka is coaxing them into doing something foolish, anything could happen. It's a troubling thought, and I rub my tired eyes, heading to my nightstand and taking a drink of day-old, cold coffee.

I'm used to staying up for days on end. Some stakeouts have had me alert for well over a day, keeping vigilant before a kill. Tracking down Luka and whatever he's planning will be no different. Especially with Delaney in danger.

Damn the girl. My heart beats faster at the thought of her, but I stride to the window where I fucked her, and I can't help but feel angry at her stubbornness. If she'd just agreed to be sent back to her parents, it would be so much easier. Nevertheless, I know part of me wants to have her close to me, to keep her in sight. I want to feel her body pressed up against mine every night, and when this is over, there will be hardly a second of spare time we have with each other that won't have my cock impaling her to the hilt.

It pulses at the thought of her, and I find myself wishing she was at my side now to work off some of this stress, but I have to keep my head clear. I'm considering relieving myself in private when I hear my cell phone speaker go off.

"Sir," one of my men says, "the blonde is on her way up to you. She seems upset."

"Noted," I grunt at my phone, raising my eyebrows. Good timing.

"Darios!" I hear Delaney's voice calling out to me as she comes up the stairs to my bedroom, and open the door to see her striding towards it, her brow knit. She's made impressive time, it would seem. She tries to storm past me into the room, but I grab her by the wrist, pulling her close to me and looking down at her with concern.

"What's the meaning of this?" I demand, glancing behind her before pulling her into my room and closing the door behind us. "What are you doing up here? I'm very busy right now, Delaney."

My gruff greeting doesn't seem to help her mood at all, and she balls her fists in frustration. I wouldn't normally be so quick to dismiss her, but I'm in the middle of trying to trace leads on this attack. Many of the Barcelona police officers I have on the take have suddenly gone quiet, and that makes me suspect a number of things — first and foremost being that local pressure is building up.

"Darios, listen to me!" she says, stepping up to me

as I glower down at her. "Why didn't you tell me Caitlin was being taken today?"

"Taken?" I repeat, arching an eyebrow. "What do you mean, has there been a kidnapping attempt? Is something wrong?"

"No," she says, stamping a foot on the ground, "I mean, ransomed! Caitlin was taken last night to be sold off to her parents and you didn't even tell me!"

I'm quick to conceal my confusion to Delaney, but this is news to me. I know we've been in contact with her parents and had planned to make the exchange sometime early this week, but none of my men had informed me that it was to be done so soon. Especially considering the fact that Lyssa's ransom is scheduled for *this morning.*

We rarely, if ever, conduct ransoms too close to one another. It doubles the risk of exposure and the parents potentially coordinating with one another or the police. And contrary to what one might think, night drop-offs are somewhat more risky than public daytime ones — we met with the Megan's parents in a public cafe to avoid just such trouble.

"Who took her?" I ask, not betraying my unease at this news.

"I...I didn't catch his name," she says, running her hand through her hair nervously as she paces about the room, "but he was kind of old, like older than most of the people here, and he looked like he had his nose broken at some point. Dark eyes?"

"Sounds like Toma," I muse, stroking my chin as I step over to the folders I have on my desk detailing some of the information about the girls and their handlers. Toma has been around for a while, but I don't remember assigning him to handling Caitlin.

"What do you mean, 'sounds like' Toma?" Delaney asks, her eyes widening as she steps over to me. "I thought you kept track of how all this goes down? Don't you know what happened to Caitlin?"

"Calm down, Delaney," I tell her in a warning tone, turning to look down at her, but her eyes are defiant and alarmed. "Toma is a trusted associate. He's been here longer than some of the other men who have handled you, you don't have anything to fear from him."

"But," she protests, putting her hands on her hips, "everything else around here happens like *clockwork*, isn't it a little weird that this would happen without you knowing about it?"

"I know what my men are up to," I say more firmly this time, taking a step towards her, my body looming over hers like a mountain. I may like this pretty little brat, but I won't tolerate my authority being questioned.

"I don't mean-" she makes an exasperated noise, rubbing her eyes and turning her back on me to stride towards the window, a fresh breeze billowing through gently. "I'm just worried that something might be going wrong. You've been overworked,

Darios, have you ever thought that you can't trust your own senses when you push it this hard?"

"Says the girl who was abducted while perfectly sober," I say, striding towards her and taking her by the shoulder, gently turning her around to face me. My expression is stony, even if my motions are gentle, and I take her chin in my hand to turn it up to me. "Delaney, I have this under control. Don't worry about it — you're overreacting."

She seems to be calming down a bit until that last word, at which she tries to pull away from me and balls her fists up again.

"Overreacting?!" she spits, "Darios, I know we're nothing but a bunch of dolled-up paychecks to you, but I know when something seems fishy!"

"You haven't been in this business as long as I have," I say, glazing over the fact that it makes the scene all the more suspect. "You don't know what you're talking about."

"Don't know what I'm-" she throws up her hands, striding around the room, her face reddening, and I suspect I've pushed her a little too far. "I am so *sick and tired* of everyone assuming I'm some dumb blonde ditz," she says, her voice thick with emotion as she teeters on the verge of tears. "You spent so much time telling me how much 'potential' and 'talent' I have, but you're just like all the others who think I'm an idiot, aren't you?"

I feel anger swelling up in my chest, and I stride

forward, a stormy expression in my eyes, and she backs up against a wall, and I put a hand beside her, trapping her under me as I glare at her. "I also told you that you're a sheltered girl who doesn't know the first thing about the real world," I say, "and this sensitivity of yours proves that!"

"Sensitivity?" she retorts, slapping my chest, "I've been sleeping with my kidnapper! I never know whether I'm going to wake up one morning and hear that the guy who's been coming inside me has decided to sell me into slavery or something!"

"Careful, girl," I warn in a menacing growl, but the next moment, Delaney breaks down into tears, melting into my arms as I hold her up.

My brow is hard for only a few moments until I find my heart softening at the sight of her, a sobbing mess in my arms, and soon, I pull her up properly and let her cry into my chest, stroking her hair gently as she lets it out.

Maybe this really is something I should be looking harder at. Above all, though, I can't risk my relationship with Delaney over something as petty as this. Well, I could, but with each passing second that I feel her melting into my arms, I feel less willing to do so.

"I spoke too rashly," I say quietly at last, hugging her to me. "It's okay, Delaney — I know you're only looking out for the people you care about. That's a rare thing among the rich. It's something you should be proud of in yourself. It's rare for people to care for others anymore."

"I care about you, too," she sobs, looking up at me with tearstained eyes, her hands gripping my shirt at my sides. "I don't want anything to blindside you, Darios."

I nod, letting a smile creep onto my face. "I care about you too, Delaney. And I understand what it's like to need to watch out for your friends. You must trust my judgement in this, but of course I would never fault you for caring too much."

She sniffs, then nods a few times, hugging me tight. "Thank you, Darios," she says, her voice cracked, and I stroke her on the back.

We stand there a moment, enjoying one another's presence, until my phone buzzes. Reluctantly, I break the hug and step over to it and raise it to my ear.

"Yes?"

"Sir," one of my men says, his voice flustered, "I've just gotten word from Officer Cardona, he checked in with us barely a minute ago."

I'm suddenly very interested, my eyes widening as I move to my map of the city. Officer Cardona is one of our officers on the take, and he was one of the few I wasn't able to get a hold of at all last night. "Well? Spit it out, what's the report?"

"We need to move, sir," says my man, sounding grim. "Cardona wouldn't leave details, but he warned that a police raid is being organized — they'll be at the compound by the end of the day."

I feel blood rising to my face, and I swear, nearly crushing the phone in my hand.

"Sir? What's the order?"

"Pack up minimal supplies and get ready to move," I say curtly, my leadership instincts kicking in. "Lyssa is set to be ransomed at noon. I want my lieutenants with me to oversee the transaction personally, and I'm bringing Delaney along for the job — nobody leaves my sight without explicit orders. I want this place a ghost town in the next half hour, do you understand me?"

"Yes, sir!" my man says, and I turn off the phone to meet Delaney's confused gaze, not having understood a word of the Georgian I was speaking into the phone.

"Hope you're ready for a new set of clothes," I tell her ruefully, putting my phone into my pocket. "We're going underground."

"We've got to leave now," Darios insists, rushing about the room collecting items into a duffel bag. His jaw is clenched and there's a sense of extreme urgency in his movements. I still don't quite understand what's going on, but just from the hurried tone of his voice when he spoke in Georgian on the phone I can tell that this is serious.

"What's happening? Why are we leaving? Where are we going?" I fire these questions at him in rapid succession, following him around the room as he packs. I am horrified to find that nearly every single drawer and nook and cranny seems to have been concealing yet another weapon, like we're on some morbid Easter egg hunt for guns.

"Have these been in here all along?!" I ask, unable to stifle the disgust in my voice. Despite the fact that

I am from a state in which hunting and weapon collecting is an accepted part of life, I have personally never been a fan. There are too many things that could go wrong in an instant. Just seeing a gun makes me feel a little queasy, to be quite honest.

"Yes," Darios answers hastily, piling the shiny weapons into the duffel bag along with several boxes of ammunition. Almost as an afterthought, he goes back to the set of dresser drawers and retrieves some clothing, as well.

"I love that weapons are prioritized over clothes. So you might be naked, but you'll be naked with a million guns," I remark, a hint of my old sarcastic wit emerging for a moment. But Darios shoots me a solemn glance and I shut up.

"If you knew the circumstances of our departure, you would not question this," he says gravely.

"Well, then, tell me what's going on. I want to know. Why are we suddenly packing up and getting out of here? Is someone coming here? Are we in trouble?" I question, holding my arms outstretched in frustration. I wish he would just be straight with me for once. I've wasted enough of my years living in between lies and deception, and it's gotten tiring. I just want to have some authenticity in my life. Even if it means hearing things I don't want to hear.

"A trusted contact has informed me of information regarding a police raid planned for this location soon," Darios explains, and I am surprised both at the content of his statement and at the openness with which he shares it. "We need to get the hell out of dodge."

"Oh my god," I murmur, clapping a hand over my mouth in horror. It's strange to realize that just weeks ago I would have been ecstatic at the prospect of the cops rushing in to save me. But something tells me that they wouldn't be here for me, anyway. This is a different situation, in which the police are not my allies.

"You understand," he says, zipping up the duffel bag and hoisting it over his shoulder. There's the frightening clatter of metal on metal as he does so, and I can't help but wince at the reminder of just how many weapons are stashed away in there.

"Okay, but you haven't answered my other question," I continue, even as he hurriedly grabs my hand and starts leading me out into the hallway, down the stairs, and out the front door. "I get *why* we're leaving, but I still don't know where the hell we're going next."

"El Raval," he answers quickly, throwing open the passenger side door of the car and helping me in, then tossing the duffel bag into the backseat before settling in behind the wheel.

"Okay... is that, like, a hotel or something?" I press him, shaking my head slowly, waiting for him to elaborate. He jams the keys into the ignition and throws the car into gear as the engine roars to life. I cross my arms a little petulantly, staring at him with my eyebrows raised. I hate when he makes me wait. I've never been an especially patient person.

"It's a slum," Darios corrects me, reaching over my lap to open the dashboard compartment. He withdraws two sets of slick designer sunglasses and a rolled-up floral scarf, tossing one pair of glasses and the scarf to me while he puts on the other pair of shades. "Put on the glasses and use the scarf to cover your hair. This will disguise us somewhat for the time being."

"A slum?" I repeat, horrified. He glances over the console at me and even though his shades completely obscure his eyes, I know instinctively that he's glaring.

"Yes, we are going there to lay low for a while," he replies. He taps the wheel impatiently and adds, "Hurry up, put it on."

"Okay, okay! I'm doing it," I shoot back, clumsily unrolling the scarf and wrapping it rather inexpertly over my head to conceal my hair and neck. Then I put on the sunglasses and turn to look at Darios expectantly. "Happy now?"

He reaches over to take my hand, a surprisingly tender gesture that knocks me off-kilter for a moment. "Yes. I do not want to risk anything happening to you," he says, his voice low and controlled. I blink at him in shock, expecting him to qualify his sweet statement with some undercutting remark, but it never comes.

"Oh," I say lamely, after a moment. "Okay."

We drive on in silence for several hours, first through the countryside and then passing within the boundaries of Barcelona, weaving through the city high-rises, lush green parks, and historical buildings.

The scenery outside my window starts to change as we move from the wealthier neighborhoods into a less-maintained area. It becomes obvious that this place isn't as cared for as the others. The buildings surrounded us on all sides down the narrow streets are still clearly ancient, pieces of history which for some reason have not been as delicately preserved. Graffiti tags mar the peeling, stained walls on either side of us, with long, spindly clothes lines hung from window to window overhead. Despite the fact that this part of the city is not given the same resources as the rest, there is still something lovely about it. Something poetic and genuine in its simple, unadorned beauty.

"Is this the place?" I ask quietly, my eyes wide as I look around.

"Yes," Darios answers simply.

We drive on for a bit longer down the tiny streets wedged between imposing structures on either side, with the occasional motorbike whizzing noisily past us, coming dangerously close to side-swiping the car. But none of this seems to bother Darios in the least, his focus totally trained on the task at hand. Meanwhile, my hands fidget nervously in my lap.

Finally, we come to a stop behind a tall, rundown building that looks to be at least fractionally leaning to one side. Worryingly so. But then Darios gets out and grabs the duffel bag, waving for me to follow him, and a feeling of heavy dread comes over me as it dawns on me that this is where we're going to be staying.

"Do you know someone here?" I ask softly, following close behind him as he pushes through the weathered door to the building.

"I know the building owner. She's an old friend. I pay her a monthly rent to maintain a small apartment here for emergency purposes," he answers with surprising candor.

"You pay rent for a place you only live in occasionally?" I question, furrowing my brow. Darios nods and leads me up several flights of rickety metal stairs. I'm thankful for my years of cheerleading, because without my athleticism this would be one hell of a journey.

"I pay for the building," he corrects, without a single fluctuation in tone.

"What?!" I burst out. "You pay for this whole rundown place? Why?"

He looks back at me over his shoulder and says, "I told you, the owner is an old friend."

"Well, if you're paying for it, aren't *you* the

owner?" I press, totally confused by the whole situation. Darios sighs and we finally stop climbing the stairs, having apparently reached our floor. He leads us down to a room at the end of the hall and takes a key out of his pocket to unlock the door.

"No. She owns it, but I pay for it. And she maintains it," he clarifies, as though it's the simplest thing in the world.

Before I can stop myself, a sardonic comment comes out of my mouth: "Does she? This place doesn't look like *anyone* is maintaining it, to be honest. If this is what you're paying her for, you might want to reconsider your arrangement."

Darios rounds on me instantly, giving me a cold look that sends a shiver down my spine, and I immediately regret my words. He pushes the door open and nudges me inside, tossing the duffel bag onto the floor and locking us in.

"My old friend is in her late sixties and she is the heart and soul of this neighborhood. She works her ass off keeping this place running. I understand that it may not live up to your spoiled daddy's girl sensibilities, and it may not be a ritzy hotel, but this is the safest place for us right now. And I will be damned if I let some snobbish American brat undermine all the hard work my friend has done here," Darios says, taking off the sunglasses to reveal his dark eyes blazing underneath.

There's less malice in his voice than expected,

though, and I get the sense that he is more disappointed than he is angry. Which, in a way, is almost worse. Rage I can handle. But the idea of doing anything to make Darios think less of me is almost too painful to bear.

"No, you're right," I reply quickly. "I'm sorry. That was really ugly of me to say. I-I guess I'm just a little scared, that's all." And that isn't a lie. I'm self-aware enough to know that the majority of my sarcasm and icy demeanor is just a guard that goes up whenever I'm uncomfortable in a situation. I don't intend to be mean. I just don't know how to respond to stress in a healthier way.

"I know," Darios says, a little more gently. "But you must learn that not all the world even wants to live the way you live. This place may not look like the pictures in your glossy travel magazines, but this is the real world, and this is where people *live*. I may have developed a soft spot for you, *patara gogona*, but I cannot tolerate unearned smugness."

"I understand. I'll work on it," I promise him earnestly, feeling sheepish. He flashes me a rare, charming smile and suddenly everything feels a thousand times better. "So, how about you give me a tour of the place," I suggest brightly.

Darios laughs. "This is about it."

I try to conceal my discomfort as I look around at our substantially reduced new digs. The apartment is essentially a studio, with a mattress on the floor in the corner, a sheer green curtain hanging over the one wide window, a miniature kitchenette with no refrigerator and only two stove burners, and a tiny bathroom with no shower, only a peeling old bathtub.

"It's, um, got a kind of quaint charm to it, doesn't it?" I comment, forcing myself to smile. Darios walks over and drapes an arm around my shoulders.

"That's the spirit," he replies. "Now, it's time we get you into some different clothes. You'll stand out here wearing that. Besides, I assume you might be a little tired of wearing the same black dress every day."

I nod vigorously. "Yes. Oh god, yes."

"Well, then, let's go," he announces. "We need to retrieve some things to make our stay a little more enjoyable, I believe."

The two of us head out into the neighborhood to visit a local market square. We spend the afternoon weaving in and out of thrift shops and discount stores, picking up soap, old linens, some towels, and toiletries for the apartment. I've been thrift shopping before, but only in the swanky hipster-esque regions of Savannah and Atlanta, so this is a whole new world for me. Darios selects some raggedy, earthy-colored clothing for me to wear while we're in the city, explaining that our best bet to stay safe is to make ourselves as unobtrusive as possible.

Besides, I have to admit that these clothes are

more comfortable than the laced-up, skin-tight designer clothing I always kept in my closet back home. And by the way Darios looks at me when I change into a brown linen peasant skirt and form-fitting, vintage white blouse, I get the feeling that he prefers me this way. Soft. Simple.

Afterward, we head to an open-air market to collect fresh fruits and vegetables, a loaf of home-baked artisan bread flavored with rosemary, and a wheel of hard, dry cheese. Darios buys an unlabeled bottle of wine from a woman in a tiny booth tucked away into an alley and I dare not question him, even though I'm a *little* concerned that we're probably buying the Spanish equivalent of bathtub moonshine. But the woman who sells it to us is so sweet and smiley that I can't help but trust her.

We head back to the apartment and spend the night eating wholesome, cheap food and settling into our new residence. Around midnight, we crack into the bottle of wine, which tastes like sugared berries and moonlight, and before long the two of us fall onto the mattress together, kissing passionately until we finally drift to sleep.

Over the next few days, Darios's guards slowly trickle back into our life, secretly moving into other apartments in the building, passing us in the hallway occasionally. Despite the fact that we're in hiding, the two of us spend most of our time outside, winding down the serpentine streets and meeting all sorts of wonderful characters. As it turns out, Darios has many friends in this part of the city, from farmers to fishermen to seamstresses. All of them seem to regard Darios with a degree of warm fondness and reverence, and a couple of them explain to me in broken Spanglish that he is somewhat of a local hero, pouring much-needed money and support into the neighborhood. Never once does Darios talk down to anyone, (except physically, because that's unavoidable with him being about the tallest man I've ever known) and I begin to see a different side of him I've only caught glimpses of before. He is kind, generous, and understanding. He listens intently to every piece of banal news and each pointless story with the same intensity I would have given a harrowing action movie. He kisses the old ladies on their cheeks, the kids on their foreheads, and shakes the hand of every older gentleman who greets him.

I find myself falling desperately, irretrievably in love with this man.

We're finally settling into the slow, simple groove of life here in El Raval when one night I leave the apartment alone to collect our clothes from the laundromat down the street. On the way back, I pass a couple of the guards standing in the doorway of one of the apartments, and overhear a whispered conversation between them.

"*Mosmena*," hisses one of the men. "Have you

heard about what happened?"

"What? What is it? I have a pot of water boiling, make it fast."

I slip into the shadows to eavesdrop, balancing the bag of clean laundry on my hip.

"About the parents who disappeared? The ones we were supposed to ransom the brunette back to? They're gone."

"The one named Caitlin? What do you mean *gone*?"

"They're nowhere to be found. I heard somebody, you know, 'took care' of them."

"That's absurd."

"No, it's true. I don't know what happened to the girl, but her parents are gone."

My heart sinks and I start to feel nauseated. I hurriedly pass by without making eye contact with either of the guards, nearly forgetting the bag of laundry in my rush to get back to the apartment. I burst into the room and Darios looks up, instantly sensing my mood.

"What's going on? Did they overcharge you or something?" he asks, looking up from the map in his hands. I hurry over to him, dropping the bag of laundry by the door.

"I just overheard two of your guards talking about Caitlin's parents going missing! Why the hell haven't you told me about this? What else are you hiding?" I shout, tears stinging in my eyes. "What happened to them? What happened to Cait? If her parents are missing, then who the hell did you ransom her out to?"

Darios gets to his feet immediately, putting his hands on my shoulders and holding me still as though to calm me down. But I can't be calmed, not when I know there's something terrible going on and my friend is in danger.

"I'm sure you must have misheard them, Delaney," he says coolly, but I detect a hint of suspicion in his tone, all the same.

"No. I didn't. Now, tell me what's going on!" I demand, stomping my foot like a bratty child.

"Delaney, listen to me. I have no idea what you're talking about. This… this wasn't my order. If something has happened to your friend or her parents, well, it wasn't sanctioned by me," Darios admits, a look of darkness coming over his handsome face.

There's a moment of quiet before I erupt into righteous fury, ripping out of his hands and crying out, "You told me not to worry! You said it was fine and I was overreacting, but I was right, wasn't I? There's another traitor out there doing this, and it's someone you know and trust, Darios. I tried to warn you. I knew something was wrong, but you just pushed me aside!"

Anger mingled with regret flashes across his features and he takes an aggressive step forward.

"Delaney, listen to me—"

"No!" I interrupt, giving him a cold stare. "You underestimated me just like everyone else does. I thought you were different, but you're not. You just see some stupid little girl when you look at me, don't you?"

"You know that's not true," Darios counters, softening his voice as he lets his arms fall to his sides. "But you're right. I should have listened to you. I didn't want to admit there could be someone working for me, one of my old loyalist crew from the war, not one of the new hired mercs, who would dare defy my orders. I let my pride blind me to the truth, and I'm sorry."

I pause, stopping myself before I could yell at him some more. The genuine apology in his voice halts me in my tracks, and I feel my rage melting away. I can't stay mad at him. Everyone has a blind spot. Even someone as powerful and imposing as Darios. I can't fault him for that.

"Okay. Fine. I-I accept your apology," I say, less bitterly than before. "But what the hell are we gonna do, Darios? I can't just stand around not knowing what Caitlin's going through."

He steps forward and pulls me into his arms, and this time I don't fight it. We stand this way for a couple minutes, just breathing in each other's comforting warmth. Then he says solemnly, "We're going to do the only thing there is to do: we're going to save your friend."

DARIOS

I hoist myself up the ladder rung by rung, making less sound than the stray cat in the alley below me as it digs through trash in the dumpster on the side of this run-down apartment complex.

If someone wants to call the south side of El Raval a slum, they can point to a building like the one I'm scaling in the middle of the night. An American eye would still recognize a European charm to it — the outside is a tan stone with very old engravings along the columns, under windows and balconies. They're simple, but distinctly Catalan. A nearby tiny balcony or window opening sports a small planter, their contents threatening to overgrow their boundaries. When the sunlight hits it just right, it might be mistaken for a decent place.

But the sunlight rarely ever hits this cramped

patch of city block, and close inspection dispels all notions of prosperity. The wiring and plumbing running along the side of the building is outdated and rusted, and there are visible patches of recent repair here and there. There's grime and stains from smoke along most of the walls, and the smell is… not pleasant. Laundry is hanging on innumerable lines between the apartment buildings. Gang graffiti is everywhere, various bands of youths making their marks on the place in invisible turf wars.

It's almost a shame to bring more violence to such a quaint Spanish slum.

The residents are not to blame for the worn down block — they never are. And the gangs are just a symptom of the real root of the problem. There is a slumlord who runs this place, leeching money off his tenants like a mosquito, leaving behind a virulent and bothersome sore. His name is Juan Palomo, and he's a step above most of the slum lords that infest El Raval like a plague.

He's my target tonight.

Palomo is well known even as far out as my villa. He got his start running predatory lending offices like payday loan operations. If the transition from lender to local crime lord can be called a transition at all, Palomo's was quick and seamless. His loan sharks got a reputation for brutality under Palomo's orders, and they soon became his enforcers. From there, it was a small step to start demanding protection money from local businesses, all from his penthouse in this trash heap of an apartment, trapping the residents under him.

He's one of the local politicians now, who's been calling for a crackdown on organized crime, amusingly enough. What a joke! Which makes me suspect him as the most likely culprit for funding the attacks on me, to secure the funding for his own anti-mob army.

A little while ago, I thought of myself as a traitor to my roots for getting such an unquenchable desire to fuck Delaney to the point of exhaustion, a hunger I still feel amidst all this squalor. But when I look at people like Palomo, I see the true class traitors — people who claw their way to the top to stand on the rubble of their fellow people.

I've studied this place from the rooftops of the surrounding buildings, and I know the routines of the gangbangers Palomo employs up on the roof of the building. As I near the lip of the roof, I ready the long knife at my side, waiting for the sound of footsteps approaching.

Three men. Palomo has been on top so long that he's relaxed, comfortable in his own home, and the three men patrolling the roof feel much the same. I hear the man nearing me pass by above, and can smell his cigarette smoke rolling down over the side of the building as I climb up after him.

He doesn't know what's hit him, from the

moment I move behind him to the second my knife plunges into the back of his head at the base of the skull. It's a quick hit, and I doubt he feels anything more than a cool sensation as I catch him and lower him to the ground.

There's an air conditioning unit on the roof that obscures the kill site from view of the rest of the guards, so I slip around to get into position for the second kill.

I feel little remorse for these people. They're long-time thugs, likely the sons of Palomo's friends doing his dirty work. They weren't forced into this life, they chose it, like my target.

But before I'm in position, the sound of a voice from one of the other thugs catches my attention. *"Miguel, tiene un encendedor?"*

Shit.

My time just became extremely precious. I hear the footsteps of the man approaching, and in a few seconds, he'll see the corpse. I pull out my silenced pistol and decide to end things quickly and deal with the risk.

I crouch and crawl over to the edge of the vent the speaker is about to come around, and the moment he appears in view, I stand up and slash his throat open with my knife. It hardly makes a sound, and before he so much as hits the ground, I drop the knife and aim the pistol at the other guard, whose back is turned to the scene.

The view of Barcelona's nighttime skyline is the last thing he sees as a soft 'thump' of his head ends his life as well.

I don't like taking such risks, but the danger of them alerting their boss to my presence is more than worth it. Without a moment to spare, I take the key to the building from one of the guards, along with my knife, and I head to the door into the top floor.

The man called Miguel was wearing similar shoes to mine, so as I descend I emulate his gait, trying to sound like him as I walk casually down the staircase. There's one guard at the base of the stairs with his back to me, thumbing through a dirty magazine. He doesn't pay me any mind as I walk down the steps, nor does he notice me in his last moments before I draw the blade and bring in swinging down into his eye socket.

I'm drawing the blade from the dead man's head when I hear a woman's gasp from the hallway, halfway to the door to Palomo's residence. My head snaps up as my heart drops. One scream could mean death for me.

The woman standing there is a middle-aged woman in an evening gown, fishnet tights, and high heels. It doesn't take a genius to deduce that she's an escort headed to Palomo's room. And she seems to know better than to try to get in the way of her clients' other business, because without making a sound, she slips out of her heels and makes for the stairwell leading downstairs.

But I'm too quick for her. Before she can reach the first step, I grab her from behind, holding a hand over her mouth.

"*Silencio*," I order her, switching to my heavily accented Spanish as I whisper the quiet order into her ear. Her eyes are wide, and she struggles for a moment in my grasp before she realizes the futility of it. "You've walked in on something terrible, miss, but you can come out alive if you follow my orders to the word. Do you understand?"

There's a pause as she processes my words, but she nods.

"*Bueno*. You were going to Mr. Palomo's quarters for your work, yes?"

Another nod.

"All I require of you is that you knock and announce your entrance as usual. You will not be harmed, and I will compensate you for every last euro lost to this job. Understood?"

She takes a deep breath and nods once more, and as I release my hand from over her mouth, I reach into my wallet and withdraw a healthy wad of cash to hand to her, which she accepts silently, a grateful nod. I get the impression that she will not miss this client's death, either.

She approaches the door, and I take my position beside it, gun at the ready. I notice an odd red mark on the hilt, and as I glance at it, I realize some of her lipstick has smudged off onto my hand.

The woman raises her fist and knocks four times at the door, raising her voice. "*Señor, su masajista está aquí.*" She's a talented actress. I would have had to crawl around the window to bypass the locked entrance, if I hadn't come upon her. The door opens after a few deadbolts unlock, and she smiles at the man in the doorframe.

Before he can say a word, I step into view with my gun raised and blow the man's brains out, a fine red spray behind him as the woman cringes away and dashes for the stairs. This time, I let her go. She's done well.

Inside, I see a few men at couches, start to get up and raise weapons, but three quick shots put them down before they can so much as take proper aim at me. I grimace at the massacre when it ends before a proper fight even starts. These slumlord's minions are easy pickings compared to the mercenaries I'm used to dealing with.

I step across the carnage of the room, expensive furniture decorated with blood, heading for the bedroom where my target waits for his meeting. My pistol was nearly silent when it went off, but I've had targets be tipped off by the sound of thumping the dead bodies make. Palomo, however, is not a man used to such professionalism.

Indeed, as I silently move down the hallway, I

hear the sound of a television playing pornography on the other side, the static-marred sounds of a woman faking an orgasm loud enough to hear through the thin wood. Under that, I can barely hear the sounds of labored breathing — a man touching himself.

Without waiting another moment, I kick the door down, and I hear a startled scream as Juan Palomo nearly pisses himself stumbling away from his bedsheets, his scrawny cock out as his white face tries to hide from me. My pistol is raised to him, and as he gets to his knees after falling off his bed, he sees all of me. And my weapon.

"*Sangre de Jesús*," he breathes, raising his hands, "Darios Esadze?!" I frown at him, looking disgusted. He's a paunchy man without a hair on his head, save for his scraggly wisps of a beard. He draws his sheets over himself in an effort to keep his dignity, but it's already long gone. I glance around the room. I can see rope and duct tape half-hidden under the bed, and I raise an eyebrow.

"My my, Palomo," I muse, "Seems you had something uncouth in mind for the lovely woman visiting you tonight."

"So the grim reaper comes for me at last," he says hoarsely, crossing himself. "Please, sir, take everything I have! I- I- had no idea I had crossed you, I wouldn't dream of such a thing in a hundred years!"

"Your very existence crosses me, Palomo," I say,

stepping around the bed and turning the TV off, sitting on the wardrobe it's perched on, gun trained on him. "But tonight, I need information from you, and if you cooperate, I'll let you hitch the next boat out of here to somewhere where you can find an honest job. I hear Corsica is lovely this time of year."

"Anything, sir!" he begs, terrified, and I want to end his pathetic life right here and now. But I must restrain myself.

"I hear you have an ear for Georgian accents," I say, narrowing my eyes at him. "You had some dealings with the Georgian mafia when we first moved into Barcelona. I need to know who else has popped up in the city who shares my proud nationality. Other Georgian gangs, Palomo, where are they?" I end on a sharp tone, pointing the gun at him meaningfully.

"O-o-other gangs?" he stammers, looking around desperately. "I don't know anything about that!"

I fire the gun at the lamp behind him, making it shatter as Palomo pisses himself. "Wrong answer, Palomo, I'm not here to play games. My compound was attacked. I know the man who led them. Red hair, missing a hand. If you don't want to match part of his description, talk."

"*Por favor, señor,*" he begs me, clasping his hands again and sobbing, "I hired a Catalan gang a few towns over! He said he could get me the money I need to wipe out my competition and secure my seat! They weren't Georgian though! I swear upon my ancestors' graves and all the saints, I know nothing more!"

When I narrow my eyes at him, he gestures around wildly. "I- I beg you, look around! You're talking to a man who's just pissed himself in terror, I have nothing to fall back on if I'm lying to you! The Georgians will have nothing to do with me since you moved in!"

As I look into his eyes, I know him to be speaking truth, as best he knows it. I curse my luck. There goes my lead.

But now I have more questions to answer. If Luka is not leading a rival gang, then what am I left with? It could not be the parents, for the mercenaries wanted the girls dead. And if Palomo knows nothing about the attack on my compound, it's unlikely Luka has merely sold himself out to some Catalan gang. What the hell is going on?

"I believe you," I say slowly, and Palomo bows his head in thanks. But none of that changes my predicament. I had grilled my own man on Delaney's suspicions, but his excuses were reasonable. And I couldn't bring myself to beat any more out of an old comrade in arms from the war. So now I've got nothing. No tie to the Georgian's after me, even if I might have the chokepoint for their money. But that's still yet to be determined.

"*Gracias*," he says, "Don Esadze, I cannot thank

you enough. You will forever have my utmost loyalty for my life this day. Bless you."

I smile, contempt growing in my heart as the color slowly leaves Palomo's face once again. "Even if I hadn't told you too much about my affairs, Palomo, you are a blight on this whole community. Many a man and woman's life has been ruined so that you can have this little throne on top of a trash heap, you know? Now tell me," I say, drawing out my knife, "what exactly did you have in mind for that poor woman you hired tonight?"

He won't be leaving here alive.

"Oh, these are gorgeous," I gasp, walking up to a vendor cart filled with local tomatoes. In contrast to the boring, uniformly smooth, lackluster red tomatoes in grocery stores back home, these vegetables are all beautifully misshapen and cast in varying hues of green, purple, and scarlet. I never knew there could be such a big difference until I came here with Darios. Over the past week I have learned to appreciate the simpler, more authentic life we've been living here. We eat better than I ever did back in Savannah, even though I dined in upscale restaurants on the regular. Everything here has more flavor, more spirit.

I know I sound like some starry-eyed hippie, but to be fair, I'm sure at least to some extent my happiness is due to the fact that I am in love.

Undoubtedly, inexplicably, in love with the man

who captured me and turned my whole world upside down and inside out. He ripped me out of my dreamlike former life, took away all my worldly possessions and power, breaking me down to recreate me anew. I only realize now how selfish I was all those years back in the States, taking everything around me for granted, pouring all my energy into something as stupid as being the most popular girl in school. Especially because guess what? High school is over. And who would I be without my legions of simpering low-rung wannabes trailing after my every word and every move? Who would I be without my imaginary crown?

As it turns out, I now know what I would be: *happy*.

Crazy, right?

Despite the impoverished conditions of our lifestyle here, and despite the fact that we're technically in hiding, with danger potentially lurking around every corner, I'm finally starting to loosen up. Strange how it took losing everything to finally become a version of myself I kind of like.

And even more strangely… I think Darios likes me, too.

We don't talk about our feelings. In fact, our emotions toward each other are just about the only topic we *don't* talk about at all. He's opened up to me about his dark, treacherous past, his childhood growing up in his native country of Georgia. He shares with me the cold, painful memories of being locked away in prison, and he's spoken about his flashbacks to the Russo-Georgian War. After hearing every bloody, torturous detail of his life, I can't help but feel a little ashamed of my own troubles. I always thought I had it bad, trying to claw my way to the top of the status quo.

But to my surprise, Darios has been oddly understanding. Underneath that jagged exterior and cold manner of speech is a charming, shockingly gentle soul. He does his best not to belittle my struggles, reminding me that context does make a difference. Still, he also keeps me on my toes, making sure I am aware of just how lucky I have been in my life thus far. I've learned so much about the world, and as a result, I've learned a lot about myself.

"Can we have caprese for dinner later?" I call out to Darios, who is talking to a vendor selling oranges. He glances over at me and winks, giving me a little nod even as he continues haggling with the mustachioed man in front of him.

I smile back at him, reaching into my pocket to pull out a few euros. I lean over the display of tomatoes, picking out three plump, juicy ones and setting them in my little wicker basket.

"*Gracias, señor,*" I tell the vendor, handing him the euros. When he tries to offer me change, I shake my head and say brightly, "Keep the change," before walking away. Passing by Darios on my way, I give him a peck on the shoulder. He pulls me close and kisses the top of my head before I can get away, giggling.

"Where do you think you're going?" he asks playfully. I bat at his arm and pull free, sticking my tongue out at him.

"Just down the street. I want to go visit Ernesto and check out his mozzarella and serrano," I reply breezily. I'm on a mission. I've already got some fantastic tomatoes, so next up is fresh cheese, dried ham, and some basil to go with the little glass bottle of local olive oil we have in the kitchen. My stomach growls just thinking about it.

"*Kargi*," Darios replies, and I've spent enough time around him to know that word means "okay." I carry on down the narrow alley, turning a corner toward the little shop owned by a friend of Darios. He always has the best selection of cured meats and fresh, creamy cheeses.

But just as I'm about to make my way onto the next street in my journey, there's a loud cough from behind me. Instinctively, I swivel around and stumble backward a step as I almost walk smack into a guy who has suddenly appeared directly behind me. He's tall and broad-shouldered, dressed to the nines, and clearly several pay grades wealthier than anyone else in this *barrio*. He would almost be rather handsome in a rubbery, talk-show-host kind of way, if not for the cruel, smug look on his overly-tanned face.

"*Hola, señorita. Haces aquí?*" he says, every syllable dripping with smarmy lewdness.

"*No te importa,*" I shoot back curtly. He simply glares down his nose at me, the smile hardening on his lips as he reaches up to swipe his fingers back through his heavily-gelled black hair.

"*Cuida tus modales,*" he growls, self-righteous fury flashing in his eyes. I see the warning signs lighting up like a beacon and I try to turn and run away, but he grabs me by the wrist and tugs me close, leaning down into my face. I can smell his hot breath on my cheek.

"Leave me alone!" I cry out, not knowing how to say it in Spanish. The man laughs derisively.

"Ahh, *ella habla ingles,*" he croons, "Just as I thought. American girl, *sí?*"

"Get your hands off of me!" I protest, trying to jerk away from him. I yelp in terror as another man suddenly comes up behind me and wraps an arm around my neck. I immediately stand still, not wanting to push these guys any further. But I have to do something. So I do the only thing I can.

"DARIOS!" I scream, with as much volume as I can muster before the second man claps a hand over my mouth.

"Shut your pretty mouth," hisses the first man. Then, he looks up at his accomplice and says, "Take her to my car and wait. I've got a little shopping to do. Make sure she's, um, *cómodo*."

Make sure I'm comfortable? I'm just beginning to frantically piece together what that could possibly mean when there's the heavy pounding of footsteps from around the corner. Darios comes bolting into the alley, and as soon as he lays eyes on what's happening, he warns, "Let her go or I will break every bone in your miserable bodies."

The wealthy man tips his head back and laughs, then looks at me with an almost piteous expression. "*Tu novio? Señorita,* you could do much better."

Darios doesn't waste another moment, rushing forward and pinning the wealthy guy's arms behind his back. The man's eyes go wide and he commands for his guard to help him. The second man immediately releases me and steps back, holding his arms up in surrender. But Darios isn't done yet.

"This will teach you not to lay a hand on that which doesn't belong to you," he snarls in the man's ear. The next second, there's a sickening crack and the wealthy man screams in pain. Darios shoves him away and the guard hurries over to help his employer, who is cradling his limp wrist and howling.

"Let's go," Darios tells me imperiously, and I follow after him. He takes my hand and we all but run back to the apartment, taking the stairs quickly in our rush to safety. And solitude.

Because now there's only one thing on my mind, and I know it's on his, too.

As soon as the door shuts behind us, Darios picks me up and pins me against the wall, peeling off his shirt and mine within seconds. I wrap my legs around his waist as he kisses me fiercely, his teeth grazing my lips and making me moan. His fingers tangle in my hair, pulling my face to one side so he can get to my exposed neck. He dives in and begins sucking heated, tingling bruises into my skin, causing goosebumps to rise along my arms and legs.

"Tell me, do you go looking for trouble, or does it simply find you wherever you go?" he whispers raspily into the shell of my ear. His warm breath sends a shiver down my spine and I feel myself getting wet, so easily manipulated by even his slightest movements.

"I think trouble has it out for me," I reply softly, and Darios pulls back to look me hard in the face, knowing that I'm referring to him and the way we met.

Without a word he pulls both of my arms up and pins them over my head with one hand, reaching down and deftly unzipping his trousers, hoisting up my skirt. When his fingers brush over my naked sex, his mouth falls open ever so slightly, his jaw going slack as he realizes that I'm not wearing any panties. Almost with a kind of animalistic instinct, he groans his appreciation, hurriedly positioning the swollen crest of his shaft at my already-slick opening. He ruts against me, his cock rubbing tantalizingly into my clit. I gasp, starting to lower my arms, but Darios stops me, pinning them back above my head.

"No. This time you're going to do exactly what I tell you," he commands in a low, gravelly tone.

I nod obediently, feeling my pussy ache with need for him.

"Who do you belong to?" he growls, leaning in to hiss the words into my ear. I'm very sensitive in that area, which he seems to know without even asking. I shudder deliciously.

"I belong to you," I answer, a little breathlessly.

"Good girl," he says, pushing into me slightly, his cock barely breaching my aching cunt. I need him to fuck me. I need him to push all the way inside and fill me up. This teasing is cruel.

"Do you want more, *chemo kargo?*" he asks, almost mocking me. I try to roll my hips forward to take more of him inside of me, but he braces me back against the wall so I can't move.

"Yes, oh please," I whimper. "I want more. I want all of you."

He gives a low, almost cruel laugh, but then he pushes slightly deeper into me and I moan. Every nerve in my body is on fire for him, begging for him to take me and make it rough. I need him to ruin me.

"Please, Darios. I need you. Tell me what I have to do," I plead, every stitch of self-conscious dignity washed utterly away in the tidal wave of my desire for him.

He doesn't answer, simply lifts me up and spears me down onto his cock, pulling away from the wall so that he totally supports my weight with ease. He wrenches my arms down and behind my back, holding both my wrists at the base of my spine as he uses his other arm to bounce me up and down on his shaft. I cry out with ecstasy as I feel the tip of his cock pistoning repeatedly into that deliciously sensitive place deep inside me, hitting it perfectly again and again until I'm arching my back and murmuring his name like some kind of filthy prayer.

"Darios, Darios," I mumble, so wrapped up in awe at how effortlessly he can hold me up and thrust into me. It's like I weigh nothing at all. He fucks into me harder and faster until tears are springing to my eyes with the overwhelming bliss of the moment, my body incapable of withstanding such pleasure, until finally I cry out as an orgasm shatters over me.

"Very good," Darios remarks, his voice thick with need, too.

He carries me over to our mattress on the floor and kneels down so that I'm straddling him, my ass bouncing up and down on his thighs. We're face to face now, and he leans forward to kiss me deeply, his hand releasing my wrists to reach up and brush the hair back from my cheeks. He carefully leans me backward so that I'm arching my back, supporting myself on my palms.

At this angle, I can feel him so deep inside me that it's almost painful, like he might tear me apart with one wrong move. But instead of fear, this thought only makes me wetter, and as soon as he starts to move against me, I have to clutch at the bedsheets.

"You feel so fucking good, *bavshvi*," he groans, pushing me back so he can reach my breasts with his lips, nipping and sucking at the soft, pale flesh there. His thrusts pick up the pace until we're both rutting against each other with abandon, grunting and moaning desperately as we both careen closer and closer to a shared release.

I lean back, giving into his relentless pace as my own pleasure threatens to rise up and swallow me whole. I'm breathing raggedly now, and Darios is grasping my hips tightly, his fingers digging into my skin. I hope it leaves a mark. I want to look in the mirror later and see the signs that he has been there, marking me as his own with purplish bruises and red lines.

Finally, he bellows my name, "Delaney!" as he shoots his hot, sweet honey deep within me, and I'm crying out only a split second later, my pussy clenching with orgasm. He wraps his arms around me and pulls me close, the two of us pressed against each other with his cock still leaking inside of me.

We stay like this for a minute or so, until there's a sharp knock at the door. I hurriedly move aside and pull the sheets up to my neck to hide my naked body. Darios stands up and quickly puts his clothes back on before answering the door. It's one of his guards.

"Darios, we have a problem," the guard says urgently.

I step out of the room with my guard, glowering at the man who interrupted my time with my woman. He's a tough man, but I stand a good head taller than him, and even he can sense the anger simmering under my surface as I glare at him and close the door behind us.

"I assume you have a good reason for interrupting me?" I say in a low tone, but my man is undeterred, steeling his nerves and nodding.

"Of course, sir, I wouldn't step in if it weren't an emergency. One of our phones received a call we weren't expecting."

"What?" I say, surprise in my voice. I'd taken precautions to ensure that we had utter privacy here, and if our phones could be traced, that meant this location might not be secure much longer. But that depends entirely on one thing. "Who got a hold of us? What do they want?"

"We can't get an ID, sir," he says hesitantly, "but I don't think it's one of our rivals. At least, not one that we know of, unless they're going through a strange middleman. It's a Frenchman."

I furrow my eyebrows, for the first time in a long time genuinely surprised as my mind races to figure out who in the hell might be calling. "A Fren-?"

I'm cut off as the door opens behind me, and Delaney's face appears in the crack of the door as I look over my shoulder at her. "Hey...um, Darios?"

"Not now, Delaney," I say calmly, putting out a reassuring hand towards her with a firm expression that says I mean it. "I'm in the middle of something."

"This is kind of urgent too," she says, her face blushing a little bit. She looks slightly pale, at the sight, I raise an eyebrow and turn to face her.

"What's the matter? You're pale, do you feel okay? Do you need something?"

"I think I'm alright," she says, glancing behind her before opening the door wider and slipping out, now fully dressed. "But do you mind if I run to the corner store across the street real quick? I just need to pick something up. I'm feeling just a little queasy."

I stare at her a moment, something nagging at the back of my mind, but finally I nod, looking to my guard again, who's been waiting patiently. "You. You will take her to the store safely. There and back, no stopping for anything else, do you understand me?"

"Of course, sir," he says, standing at attention as though we're back in the Special Forces together. I smile.

"Good man. I'll have your teeth if you fail me," I add, half-jokingly. "Now this call-"

"He's still on the line, in the room across the hall," he says, gesturing to a door not far from here. I chuckle.

"I must be an important man for him to be so patient. Alright, off, both of you, go," I say, ushering my guard away, and Delaney gives me a grateful smile as I pause her a moment to give her a kiss, and our eyes linger on one another for a couple of moments. She knows this isn't something I would have allowed her in the not-so-distant past. Strange to think how far we've come since we've first met. Yet as we break our gaze and she runs off with my guard, I can't shake an odd feeling in the pit of my stomach.

Nevertheless, I step into the room indicated to me, where I see a number of my guards standing around a phone on the table. My lieutenant gives me a relieved look as I step in, and without hesitation, I pick up the phone and put it to my ear.

"You're a brave man," I muse in French, putting my other hand into my pocket as I stride over to the filthy window of the place while my men watch from behind. My eyes scan for shady vans or signs of gunmen, but the din of the streets is the same as ever.

"You're a careful man!" comes a higher-pitched Frenchman's voice from the other end of the line. "Do you have any idea how hard you are to get a hold of? El Raval on the first day, a dead slumlord the next! Ha! Here I was starting to think the illusive Darios Esadze was going soft, but you can swim with the sharks as good as ever. It was tempting to use the office equipment to track you, but keeping this off the official record let me flex my skills a little, so thanks for that, I guess."

I hold the phone away, making a face at it in confusion. "You talk too much," I finally say curtly.

"Well, you know, the suits at INTERPOL get a little dull to work with from time to time," the man says, and my eyes widen. If the international European police force is interested in my activities, then things are in hotter water than I thought. "Don't worry," the voice quickly adds, "you're not on their radar, not in a big way, at least. In fact, we're a little grateful to you for dealing with Palomo. But when I saw your name come up, I just had to get a hold of the one man my friend Maksim couldn't kill."

That name hits me like a sack of bricks, and my eyes widen. That's a name I haven't heard in a long time. There could only be one man he's referring to: Maksim Pavlenko was a Russian hitman with the Bratva in France. Every bit as tough as me and every bit as fierce. We crossed paths what feels like a lifetime ago. I got someone's attention when I was still a small fry, and there was a hit taken out on me. I escaped and laid low for a while, but Max is responsible for one of the scars on my body. Just as I'm responsible for one of his, I recall with some measure of pride. There's something to be appreciated about another hitman's work, just as there is in giving one a wound he'll remember.

"Who is this?" I ask slowly, my tone measured.

"Call me Felix," says the flippant voice on the other end, "I'm a friend of Max. Oh, and don't worry about him anymore, he dropped the Bratva like a hot potato."

"You're both bold and strange," I remark, glancing back at my men, most of whom don't speak French as well as me and can't follow the conversation closely.

"Yes, well," Felix muses, "you're not the first hitman to tell me that. But I'm not keeping out of official channels just for personal reasons," he goes on, his voice getting more serious. "I've done a little digging on this case of yours, the raid on your compound."

"How do you know about that?"

"Well, for one, I'm good. For two, because there

are police records of it — as in, *it was ordered by the police*, Mr. Esadze."

My face goes red, and I feel my jaw clench against my will. "The police. Are you sure?"

"Well, I *am* the police, I guess, so yeah. But this comes from a more local police force, not INTER-POL. Spanish authorities paid for those mercenaries, through a healthy chain of mediums to make sure everything was kept quiet."

"*What?*" I rasp, my voice thick with anger. If this is true... "The mercenaries were after blood when they attacked! Are you trying to tell me the government wants those girls dead?"

"That's exactly what I'm telling you," Felix says grimly. "I'm afraid it's not that unusual. Poor children going missing in the sex trade is just a statistic, small potatoes to the international community. But a handful of rich daughters get taken? That's worth some attention. Ah, but what's worth more? A few rich daughters *getting killed* in violent gang warfare."

I feel my blood boiling as Felix's explanation lets the pieces fall together in my mind.

"The government wants a violent end to the hostage situation," he says. "If those rich American girls turn up dead, the media will go crazy, it'll be a feeding frenzy. And American money will come pouring into Spain to help drive out eastern European gangs like you Georgians."

"And the money lines the pockets of the richer officials," I say with a grimace.

"Spot-on, big guy," Felix says. "If I were you, I'd hightail it out of the country and lay low with whoever you've got left. And I say that just because you and I both know how despicable it is for these rich fucks to make a buck off innocent lives."

I let out a low murmur of agreement, not glad to have my suspicions confirmed. "Thank you. If you run into Maksim again, tell him I won't try to kill him."

Felix gives a low whistle. "Damn, high praise. I'm not saying I'll stick my neck out for you, so don't get cozy."

"Don't make things *too* easy on me," I say bemusedly, and before Felix can answer, the door bursts open, and all our heads turn to the doorway, hands going to the guns at our sides.

But in the doorway is not an enemy. It's the guard I sent with Delaney, clutching a bullet wound in his chest and looking at us with a face strained in pain.

"Sir! Delaney!" His voice is choked with agony as blood pools at his feet. "A black van, they...they took her! There were too many, I..." his voice becomes faint, and my men rush to his side as he collapses.

I wake with a start as the world around me jolts violently. Was I asleep? I thought I was walking down the street with one of the guards. Where the hell am I? Why is everything so dark? I try to open my eyes, but there seems to be something pressing against my eyelids, like there's a blindfold wrapped around my head. I try to speak, but my throat feels rough and I'm too weak and tired to summon my vocal cords into action. And when I attempt to lift my arms, I find that they are bound behind me, my shoulders and wrists aching painfully.

Even with my senses numbed down to nearly nothing at all, my brain slowly wakes up and pieces together that wherever I am, I'm sitting down — but still moving. The world is moving. Fast.

I listen hard and notice the whirring of an

engine and the familiar crunch of tires rolling down dirt roads. Back in Georgia, my parents have a vacation home in the foothills we used to visit all the time in the summer when I was a child, and my bleary mind automatically transports me back to the memories of riding along in the backseat as our tricked-out Jeep rumbled down the long dirt roads to the house. That's exactly what it feels like right now, except that instead of excitement and anticipation, it's terror that's spurring my heart to beat ever faster.

Where the hell am I going?

And who's taking me there?

"She's waking up," mumbles a male voice somewhere in the vicinity. I gasp in fear and move my head around, helplessly searching for the source of the sound, in vain. I can't see anything with this strip of fabric tied across my eyes, and my head is pounding. It almost feels like a hangover — but a thousand times worse. A wave of nausea builds up in my chest and I have to swallow back the bile rising in my scratchy throat.

What did they *do* to me?

"Nice of you to join us," quips another, louder male voice. There's a certain cockiness to his tone that sets me on edge. "We're almost there. Have a nice nap?"

"P-Please, help me," I manage to croak out, not even sure why I'm saying it. I may not know my location or my company, but I sure as hell know there's nobody here who's going to help me.

There's a faint round of cruel laughter and then the cocky voice continues, "Oh, too late for that, I'm afraid. Nobody is going to save you this time. But don't worry, you're going to see your friend very soon. We've got a sweet little reunion planned for you, just wait and see."

"Turn here," instructs another voice, and I can vaguely sense the vehicle turning around a corner, and the car moves more slowly now, obviously coming to a halt somewhere up ahead. When it finally stops, I feel a pair of rough, calloused hands grab hold of my shoulders and I yelp in panic. Wordlessly, I am dragged out of the vehicle and set on my feet. But I'm still wobbly and weak from whatever these guys did to me, and I nearly collapse as soon as my feet touch the ground.

"Whoa, there," says the man holding me up.

"Take her inside," orders the arrogant voice. "Feel free to take off the blindfolds once you're there. I want her to know exactly who is going to end her life. I want her to see every detail."

"Wh-what?" I choke out, turning my head toward the voice. But the man behind me is already half-carrying me across the rocky, dirt road and through a doorway. My feet drag along what feels like cold concrete, and I assume we're either in a warehouse or perhaps some kind of abandoned farmhouse.

There are enough of the latter back home in Georgia that I am well-acquainted with the surroundings. There's even still the faint scent of hay and rotting wood.

"Please, I want to see," I murmur weakly, and the man behind me sighs exasperatedly before ripping off my blindfold. I blink in the sudden onslaught of harsh light, my headache worsening instantly. I wince, but I force myself to open my eyes again, squinting around at the room I've been dragged into.

It's definitely an old farmhouse. There are big stalls once used to house horses and cattle, and the dark red paint on the wooden walls is peeling off in blistered strips.

"Why am I here? Who are you people?" I whisper. The man simply shoves me down into a stall, shutting and locking the gate behind me as I fall to the filthy floor. But instead of clattering down to the hard concrete, I land on something soft — and shivering. I turn to see that I've landed on a person.

A familiar, though somewhat gaunt, face peeks back at me.

Caitlin!

"Oh my god," I murmur. She has tear-stained streaks down her face and her hair is all matted, but it's definitely her.

"I was so wrong," she whimpers into my ear. "I messed up, Laney."

"What about your parents?" I ask, pushing back

and staring into her face. She shakily raises one arm to point to the stall next to us.

"They're here, too. Right over there. These guys kidnapped them, too. They — they say they're going to kill all four of us. They were just waiting for you," she explains, fresh tears welling up in her brown eyes.

"No," I breathe, shaking my head. "No, I-I won't let that happen."

But my heart is hammering away in my chest and I know deep down that there's nothing I can do. It's clear that even Caitlin, my eternally sassy and spirited best friend, has given up entirely. There's no trace of her former spark remaining; all that she has left is sadness as she awaits a certain death.

"It's over, Laney," she murmurs, falling into my arms.

"She's right, you know," remarks a cold, cocksure voice from behind me. I look back over my shoulder to see a tall, pale man with curling red hair, dressed in all black. He's leaning on the gate and smiling down at us viciously, like a shark circling its helpless prey.

"Why? Why are you doing this? And who are you?" I ask, heaping as much venom as I can manage into my tone.

He rolls his eyes. "None of that really matters, but since you ask — we're doing this because there's no better way to make money and cause a media frenzy than to execute four Americans on foreign soil. Once the authorities get their hands on the video we're going to make… well, let's just say you'll all be famous."

"Please don't do this," I beg softly.

The man tilts his head to one side, glaring down at me with a slight look of bemusement on his pale face. "You know, it would be a shame to let such a beautiful girl go to waste. That one over there doesn't have any fight left in her, so that wouldn't be much of a good time. But you, oh I can tell you would so much fun to break."

My blood runs cold when I realize what he might be hinting at. "I could show you things you've never felt before," he goes on, opening the gate and kneeling down slightly to gaze into my eyes.

"Don't touch me," I retort, spitting into his face. He winces and swipes at his cheek, smiling down at me with renewed ferocity.

"Ooh yes, that's the kind of spirit I like to see. It would be such a pleasure to wring that attitude right out of your pretty little body," he says, reaching down to cup his crotch lewdly. "How about it, my little whore? Want to have a little party before the execution? Just you and me?"

Caitlin's hand tugs on my arm protectively, but I stand up in front of her, shielding her with my body and staring up defiantly into the redhead's face. He sneers down at me.

"Eager, are you? Come with me," he says, snatching me around the waist. He drags me out of the stall and shoves me to the ground. "Get on your knees!" he shouts, snapping his fingers impatiently.

Before I can even fully process the situation, there's an ear-splitting bang as the door to the barn house opens and bullets zing through the air. Two of the men several yards away fall to the ground. The red-haired man turns on his heel and ducks down to the ground, heaving me into his lap to use me as a sort of human shield. This position, while horrifying, gives me a full view of the situation at hand.

Namely, the fact that Darios is bolting onto the scene with a pistol in one hand and a knife in the other. The red-haired man shouts from behind my shoulder, "Bastard!"

Another two guards come running from the back and Darios fires a round at one and hurls the knife at the other. Just like that, they're dead on the ground and Darios has only a split second to turn his gun on Redhead before they're on top of each other, grappling.

Darios doesn't fire the gun so close, not with us in danger of getting hit by a ricocheting bullet, but my captor doesn't have any such qualms, and he gropes for the gun vigorously while they struggle.

"Luka, you fucking traitor," Darios growls in Georgian, and I realize I've picked up a little of the language over my time among the men. But

Redhead, who must be Luka, says something back that I can't understand, and he brings a quick punch around to the side of Darios's head. Strangely, I hear the sound of metal connecting with his jaw, and he's knocked away from Luka, reeling, and to my terror, I hear a clatter on the ground and realize that his gun has been knocked out of his hand. My breath catches in my throat as I watch Luka hold up Darios's own knife with a grin and prepares to dive forward again.

"You should have killed me when you had the chance, Darios," the man taunts in English, glancing at me with a cruel smile. "Maybe I'll take *your* hand before I take your girl."

"You should have taken my warning," Darios retorts, "I've grown less merciful over the years." With that, Luka lunges.

This time, though, Darios is ready for him, and he catches Luka's wrist, jerking it down and pulling the man's whole body along with it as he delivers a quick, strong jab to his throat. I hear the sound of him choking as he hits the ground. Darios's body is as deadly unarmed as it is without weapons, and he delivers an ax kick to Luka's back, knocking the wind out of him.

I watch Darios's eyes flit to the wall nearby, where some old farming tools, rusted with age, are lying. His muscular arms reach for something, but my eyes are drawn to Luka's furious, bloodshot eyes as he reaches to his side, drawing out his gun with terrifying speed.

"Darios!" I cry out, but before I can shut my eyes to await the inevitable...there' the sound of metal sinking into flesh as Darios drives an old pitchfork into Luka's neck, paralyzing him with wide eyes and a jaw hanging open as blood pools in his mouth and trickles out, the gun falling uselessly to his side.

Darios steps back, letting the pitchfork loom over the body like a gravestone while I let out a cry and run forward, and he catches me in his arms, lifting me off my feet as he brings me into a tight hug.

"Shush now, darling," he says, that hot accent making my soul melt as I feel wave after wave of relief washing over me, "did you really think I'd let that rat kill you?"

"I thought I'd never see you again," I sob into his shoulder, "and that was the most horrible thought of all!"

"You were right all along, Delaney," he says, setting me down and looking at me sincerely, a smile on that hardened killer's face. "I won't make the mistake of disregarding your words again." Tears roll down my eyes as I hug him tight, never wanting to let go, and he kisses my forehead before looking up at Caitlin and her family, who have been cowering against the wall, only now starting to cautiously stand up.

"Is it...is it over?" Caitlin's mother asks, her voice shaky.

"Yes," Darios says, holding me to his side like a war trophy, and it feels so right. "All of you are free now — your ransoms are null, consider them forgotten. Go back to your homes and forget my face. You all, you have lives to get back to."

I wrap my arms around Darios's waist, looking up at him with shining eyes, my heart filled with both adrenaline and admiration, utmost love for this dominant killer who's claimed me and doled out vengeance in a single motion. "And *we* have a life to start," I say, and he grins down at me, the Georgian showing in that devilish smile of his before he kisses me on the lips.

"Indeed we do *chemo kargo*. After all," he says, leaning in to whisper into my ear as I feel a tingle run through my whole body, "I did tell you I might keep you for myself."

My axe sinks into another log, and the smell of freshly chopped wood fills the air as the two halves of lumber fall to the ground with a solid 'thunk.' I wipe the sweat from my brow, smiling at the gracious forest breeze blowing gently over my bare chest as I turn my eyes to the car coming up the dirt road.

Delaney is pulling up in the new Fiat I bought her a few months ago. It isn't my first choice of cars, but I told her I'd get her whatever she liked when we moved, so a Fiat it was. I didn't think a new car was exactly the most fitting for a new leaf in our new, more rustic residence, but there are a few creature comforts I find myself unable to deny the woman.

She steps out of her car with an anxious smile on her face, her swollen belly giving her some trouble as she stands up, and I approach her to wrap my arms around her waist. As I do, her anxiety melts away, and she meets my kiss with a gentle sigh.

"Welcome home, my love," I say, putting my forehead to hers as she grins like an embarrassed school girl. "How did the meeting with your parents go? You're here, so I can't imagine it went too terribly."

I start to lead her into the cottage I built for her as I talk. It's a quaint little place, made from wood and stone I either obtained with my own hands or bought from the village a few kilometers away from here. We're well out of the way from the hustle and bustle of life, and I've been teaching Delaney the basics of subsisting off one's own land while we're out here.

"It went...okay," she says as I hold open the wooden door for her, letting her walk into the surprisingly spacious wooden interior, a crackling fire at the far end of the room and the smell of freshly cooked Spanish gazpacho filling the room a pot by the fire. Delaney smiles as she enters, taking in the aroma as I watch the worries of the day melt away.

"I didn't expect them to be thrilled by the idea of you starting a life with a man like me," I chuckle, rubbing her back gently with a large hand that's been growing even rougher by the day as I work our land. "Especially considering your change of scenery."

"They aren't happy, no," Delaney admits, turning

to face me as she strokes her stomach, and I do the same, feeling our daughter kick in the womb, filling me with joy. "But I'm already pregnant, and they know how I feel about you — how we feel about each other," she says, a confident smile growing on her face. "So it's not the ideal life *they* had planned for me, but they've come to peace with the fact that it's going to happen."

"They can count on that," I say, lowering my voice as I take her chin in my hand and plant a kiss on her lips before I whisper into her ear. "If they thought they could keep you from me, they should remind themselves I'm perfectly happy to kidnap you all over again."

I feel a shiver go up her body, and her eyes grow lidded as she looks up at me, her hands working up my impeccable sides.

We're living in the midst of a Spanish forest together, the nearest city being Barcelona, though even that is a long way from where we are. To my great surprise after we agreed to live together and start a life, it was Delaney who suggested getting away from the hustle and bustle of the big city.

There's been a real change in her since she's been in my company. She talks so much less about the empty pursuits of material goods and pastimes of the rich folk. The idea of getting closer to nature seemed to excite her, and with each passing day, she seems to enjoy herself more and more. The prospect of raising a little girl away from the cutthroat and wasteful culture she was brought up in seems just as exciting to her. She'll finally have a chance to give her daughter — *our* daughter — the upbringing she never had but always wanted.

It's all something new for me, too. Never in my wildest dreams did I think I'd fall in love, much less with a girl like Delaney, but since we've been together, we've grown into each other so much that I can't imagine life without her.

I still have many connections in the mafia, and I still have not decided what will become of my little operation running out of that old villa in Barcelona, but right now, my thoughts are utterly consumed by the life I want to give Delaney and our daughter. My heart swells with pride at the thought that she'll grow up in a world far from the hardship I knew, far from the violence of war and the ravages of poverty.

In the meantime, though, every night with Delaney has been filled with passion. If I fucked her wantonly and with abandon in the middle of our crisis, my lust for her has only been fanned by the quiet, and not a night passes without her cries of bliss as my solid cock rocks her whole body.

And on our honeymoon across Spain, I spent so much time inside her I hardly noticed the sights around us. She didn't seem to mind.

She keeps up with her friends — Megan, Caitlin, and Lyssa, all three of them now safe and sound back in America. She tells me all of them are doing well, though most of them are going right back to the lives they were stolen from so briefly. Caitlin, however, had more of an impression made on her than the rest, and Delaney seems to be keeping up with her more than the others. She tells me the girl isn't so willing to let the government corruption she witnessed go unanswered, and I hear she's studying for law school to face it head-on.

I never heard again from the INTERPOL agent, and I prefer things to remain that way. Out here, I'm largely off the grid, out of the public and international eye. I'd be surprised if even the mafia can find me, if I don't want to be found. Retiring is a thought that's crossed my mind a few times — I certainly have the savings to do so and still live *very* comfortably with Delaney and our budding family. I certainly don't plan on ransoming young girls anymore, but I worry that my men would feel lost without my direction, so I may keep up an adminis-trative role from a distance, ensuring the Georgian presence in northern Spain is protected and respected.

Only time will tell.

"If that's on the table," she says, turning those endless blue eyes up to me, "then maybe I ought to try to run away again."

I grin down at her. "Don't try me, girl," I say in that same growl I used when I first claimed her, and she arches her back into me. "But first..." I say, gently nodding back outside, "I have a surprise for you."

She tilts her head to the side, following me as I walk back out the door. I have a workshop detached from the cottage, where I've taken up carpentry and woodworking as something of a trade. It came naturally as I started to build our homestead, and I found myself with a natural talent for it. That, and it is incredibly relaxing.

Delaney follows me inside, the smell of wood and varnish filling our senses, and her eyes widen at what she sees fresh off the bench, and she throws her arm around me with a delighted squeal. "Oh my god, Darios, it's beautiful!"

I've made a crib from scratch, a sturdy thing made from mahogany wood and embellished with designs I remember from my homeland, where tradesmen are valued artisans. I've managed to keep it hidden for a week or so while I worked on it, but it's finally finished, and I must say, it came out very well.

"It's the pride and joy of my work," I say, crossing my arms and gazing at it. "Only the best for the pride and joy of our love," I say, smiling down at my young bride. As she hugs me tight, I can feel her heart pounding against me, our love like an aura of peace in this remote, serene, rustic place.

"I love you so much, Darios," she says, her voice quiet, and I squeeze her against me.

"I've never loved anything in this cold, harsh world as much as you, Delaney," I reply, looking down at her with a warmth I didn't know I had in me. "I will prove that to you every day. I stole you from the gilded world of the rich, but tell me — are you happy away from it all?" I lift her face to mine, true concern on my face. "Would you be happier back in the city? Madrid? Barcelona? Seville?"

She buries her face in my chest, a soft giggle escaping her chest. "Those all sound like great places to go on a vacation now and then," she muses before looking up at me as I run my hand through that light golden hair that I could get lost in forever, my other hand squeezing that firm ass that spoons into me every night. "But everything I've been through, every interesting thing about my life...I feel like it only started after I met you. I never want to go back to that old life."

I kiss her deeply, all our worries miles and miles away into oblivion, the only thing that matters right here in this room. "As you wish, princess," I tease, and she slaps my chest laughing as I wrap my arms around her, my own deep chuckle in harmony with hers as I pepper her face with kisses.

As she steps forward to let me show her some of the finer details of the handiwork, a bird on the windowsill chirps, the sound of it and the gentle rustle of the forest just outside reminding us that at last, we can live together in peace, that we can make our own future in any way we want.

Together.

* * *

THANK you so much for reading! I hope you enjoyed <3 If you have a moment, please leave a review. Other readers are dying to know what you thought.

I have plenty more bad boy romance for you, including the rest of the Hitman Series, so make sure you check out my other books on the next couple of pages, and sign up for my newsletter to be notified when I have a new release on the way!

Owned by the Hitman
Ebook | Audiobook | Paperback

Sold to the Hitman
Ebook | Audiobook | Paperback

Saved by the Hitman
Ebook | Paperback

Captive of the Hitman
Ebook | Paperback

Stolen from the Hitman

Ebook | Paperback

Hostage of the Hitman
Ebook | Paperback

Taken by the Hitman
Ebook | Paperback

GLOSSARY

GEORGIAN

- *genatsvale* : untranslatable term of endearment, something like "you before me"
- *Dila mshvidobisa* : Good morning/afternoon (greeting)
- *chemo kargo* : my good one (term of endearment)
- *sykhaara* : my light (term of endearment)
- *dampalo dzaghlo* : rotten dog (expletive)
- *chemo okro* : my gold (term of endearment)
- *bavshvi* : baby (term of endearment)
- *Mshvidad iqavi* : Be quiet
- *Nabozvaro* : Bastard (insult)
- *Ghmerto chemo* : My god

- *patara gogona* : little girl
- *Diakh* : Yes
- *ghmert'i* : oh god
- *Mosmena* : Listen

SPANISH

- *¡Cuatro cervezas, por favor!* : Four beers, please!
- *Con un limón, también* : With a lemon, also
- *la ensalada con fresas y un té, por favor* : The salad with strawberries and a tea, please.
- *¿tiene un encendedor?* : got a lighter? (cigarette lighter)
- *silencio* : silence
- *bueno* : good, okay
- *Señor, su masajista está aquí* : Sir, your masseuse is here
- *Sangre de Jesús!* : blood of Jesus!
- *Por favor, señor* : please, sir
- *Hola, señorita. Haces aquí* : Hello, miss. What are you doing here?
- *No te importa* : It's none of your business/It doesn't matter to you (colloquial)
- *Cuida tus modales* : Mind your manners
- *Tu novio* : Your boyfriend

ALSO BY ALEXIS ABBOTT

<u>Romantic Suspense:</u>

HITMEN SERIES:

Owned by the Hitman

Sold to the Hitman

Saved by the Hitman

Captive of the Hitman

Stolen from the Hitman

Hostage of the Hitman

Taken by the Hitman

The Hitman's Masquerade (Short Story)

THE KILLER TRILOGY:

Book 1: Killer for Hire

Book 2: Killer Desire

Book 3: Killer on Fire

SEXY SEALs

Sweetheart for the SEAL

Sights on the SEAL

HOSTAGES:

Stealing Her

The Assassin's Heart

Killing For Her

Abducted

STEPBROTHERS:

Ruthless

Criminal

STANDALONES:

Betting on Love

Hunter's Baby

I Hired A Hitman

Vegas Boss

Rock Hard Bodyguard

Innocence For Sale: Jane

Redeeming Viktor

Romance:

Falling for her Boss (Novella)

Most Wanted: Lilly (Novella)

Bound as the World Burns (SFF)

Erotic Thriller:

THE **D**ANGEROUS **M**EN **S**ERIES:

The Narrow Path

Strayed from the Path

Path to Ruin

ABOUT THE AUTHOR

Alexis Abbott is a Wall Street Journal & USA Today bestselling author who writes about bad boys protecting their girls! Pick up her books today if you can't resist a bad boy who is a good man, and find yourself transported with super steamy sex, gritty suspense, and lots of romance.

She lives in beautiful St. John's, NL, Canada with her amazing husband.

facebook.com/abbottauthor

twitter.com/abbottauthor

instagram.com/alexisabbottauthor

bookbub.com/authors/alexis-abbott

pinterest.com/badboyromance

youtube.com/AlexisAbbott

CONNECT WITH ALEXIS

Get an EXCLUSIVE book, **FREE** just as a thank you
for signing up for my newsletter! Plus you'll never
miss a new release, cover reveal, or promotion!

http://alexisabbott.com/newsletter

facebook.com/abbottauthor

twitter.com/abbottauthor

instagram.com/alexisabbottauthor

bookbub.com/authors/alexis-abbott

pinterest.com/badboyromance

ACKNOWLEDGMENTS

Thank you to my amazing Patrons. I'm constantly humbled and grateful for your support.

Ramona Cabrera
Melissa Hedrick
Virginia Swanson
Dawn Daughenbaugh
Don Doss
Stacie Currie

If you'd like to join them — and get my ebooks or paperbacks — you can find me here on Patreon.
https://www.patreon.com/alexisabbott

www.ingramcontent.com/pod-product-compliance
Lightning Source LLC
Chambersburg PA
CBHW061603190726

48288CB00007B/2157